KU-735-102

ECO WORRIERS: TREE TROUBLE

Kathryn Lamb

First published in Great Britain
in 2008 by
Piccadilly Press Ltd
This Large Print edition published
by AudioGO Ltd 2011
by arrangement with
Piccadilly Press Ltd

ISBN 978 1405 663823

Text copyright ©
Kathryn Lamb 2008

The right of Kathryn Lamb to be
identified as Author and Illustrator
of this work has been asserted by her
in accordance with the Copyright,
Designs and Patents Act, 1988

All rights reserved

British | 05/13 RYE **EAST SUSSEX** | available

	EAST SUSSEX	
	03653357	
AudioGO	01.12.10	
9|13 For	£9.99	
12|10	CR02 J	

Printed and bound in Great Britain by
CPI Antony Rowe, Chippenham and Eastbourne

For Jasper, Safia, Lexus, Lunah and Juliette—and their parents

CHAPTER ONE

WHUMMP! With one massive sideways thwack from her pillow, Evie fells me like a tree across my bed. I am laughing too much to get up again, so she brings down the pillow with a soft thwump on my shoulder, and collapses, giggling, on the bed beside me.

Evie and I like to have sleepovers together—we only live two doors away from each other along Frog Street. But we are not allowed a sleepover tonight as it is the first day of the autumn term tomorrow. So instead of our usual Eco-Worriers' Night In Pillow Fight, we have just had a special Last Night of Freedom Before the Day of Doom Pillow Fight.

'I'll have to go home soon,' Evie sighs. 'Mum told me not to be late on pain of death or doing all the washing-up for a week.'

'It's not that late!' I protest. 'I could walk with you.'

We pass Mum on the landing, sorting out my school uniform.

'Is it OK if I walk Evie home, Mum?'

'Yes—but come straight back.'

I nudge Evie with my elbow. 'Stop staring!' I whisper.

'I can't help it!' Evie giggles as we make our escape. 'Your mum looks like an emo—only not as scary.'

This is true. Mum's hair has changed colour at regular intervals this year, and yesterday she dyed it jet black.

'If she starts getting piercings and wearing thick black eye-liner, I am moving OUT!' I groan.

*   *   *

At Evie's house, her mum and dad are sitting at the kitchen table, poring over travel brochures.

'You are sooo lucky!' I sigh. 'I wish I was jetting off to the sun at half-term. Couldn't you hide me in your luggage, or something?'

'I wish I could!' Evie exclaims, fishing two organic strawberry-and-mango smoothies out of the fridge.

'I'm sorry, Lola,' says Evie's mum, looking up from her brochure. She has the same mass of red curls as Evie, and the same green eyes. 'We thought we'd have a family holiday before Liam has to knuckle down to some serious revision. Perhaps you could come with us next time.'

'Oh, yes!' I reply, nodding. 'That would be great.'

We take our smoothies up to Evie's room. Big dark clouds have rolled across the sky, and a light drizzle is misting the window panes.

'I bet you can't wait to swap weather like this for all that sunshine!' I say, trying not to be jealous.

'You're right—I can't wait!' Evie enthuses, her eyes shining. Then, with an unconvincing attempt to look serious, she says, 'Of course, I'm concerned about all those aeroplane fuel emissions literally sending our carbon footprint rocketing sky-high, so I'm going to plant a tree.'

I raise my eyebrows. 'Will that help?' I ask.

'Of course it will. That's what

everyone does these days. If you go on a plane, you should plant trees to offset the carbon emissions, because trees reabsorb some of the CO_2 which your flight has belched into the atmosphere.'

'So if you're always going on planes, do you have to plant a whole forest?'

'Probably.'

We sip our smoothies through recyclable straws. Evie reaches the loud slurrrp at the bottom of the carton first.

'I'd better go,' I say. 'Mum told me to come straight back—I'd better not wind her up or she might put a spell on me. She already looks like she's dressed up for Halloween. Did you notice she was wearing black to match her hair?'

Evie laughs. 'Oh, come on! She doesn't look that bad!'

We pass Evie's brother, Liam, on the stairs. I can only see his dark hair as he has his nose buried in a magazine and doesn't appear to notice us.

'Since when has Liam been reading women's magazines?' I can't help asking, as we leave the house—Evie has asked her mum if she can walk me home.

'Oh, don't worry about it,' Evie replies, breezily. 'I know it's weird. But Liam's weird. He's obsessed with some supermodel called Jadene, and there's an article about her in Mum's magazine. He's even got pictures of her on the wall in his room.'

'Airhead Amelia's always raving about Jadene,' I remark. 'She brought in loads of magazines at the end of last term and was bragging to her friends about how her mum and dad know all these celebrities, including Jadene. Then she said that she was going to be a supermodel just like Jadene when she leaves school.'

Evie snorts derisively. 'Fat chance!' she exclaims.

Neither of us likes Amelia very much, especially since her dad, David Plunkett, a successful businessman, tried to get the Ecological Gardens closed down. He wanted to buy up the land and expand his horrible Plunkett's Plastics business. Amelia and her mum, a journalist, were involved in spreading ugly rumours about the Eco Gardens. Evie and I managed to expose the Plunkett plot, and the sanctuary was saved. Amelia was furious, and now she never misses an opportunity to be mean and spiteful to us.

'It seems like ages since we helped save the Eco Gardens,' Evie says. 'But it's only been a few weeks. We actually got to speak to Dodo—or should I say "squeak" to her—because I was so nervous I couldn't actually speak! Did I look like a complete idiot, Lola?'

'As I've told you a hundred times, Evie—no.'

Dodo is our favourite singer, and she gave a concert at the Eco Gardens last week after Kate Meadowsweet, the principal keeper of the gardens, took up our suggestion to invite her. The concert was sold out and raised loads of money for the Pablo Appeal to save wildlife and stop global warming.

'It was soooo cool!' I say dreamily.

We have reached my house after d-a-w-d-l-i-n-g in our usual manner between houses in order to have time to talk. We hover in the hallway, reminiscing about our exciting summer.

Mum comes out of the kitchen, and I ask her if I can walk Evie home again. She gives me a look which I interpret as 'no'. I decide that her new incarnation as a kind of emo mum has definitely made her look scarier. Evie obviously feels the same way and leaves hurriedly after saying that she will meet me in the morning as usual to walk to school.

I find Dad in the living room, watching TV. I decide to have a go at him about holidays.

'Evie's family are taking her to the Costa Fortuna Sunshine Resort for half-term,' I remark, pointedly.

To my surprise, Dad doesn't erupt like some kind of human volcano, spewing out stuff about how money doesn't grow on trees and he has bills to pay and so on— I have often thought of harnessing Dad's occasional outbursts of anger to a power generating station as a source of alternative energy—but instead he gives me a slight smile. 'I'm not promising anything,' he says, 'but you

7

may be in for a nice surprise in the not too distant future.'

Oh, wow! Does this mean what I think it does? Sunshine Resort, here I come! I fly across the room and give Dad the hugest of hugs.

'Oh, thanks, Dad! You're the best! And I promise I'll plant at least ten trees!'

Dad looks faintly surprised. 'Er— OK, love. Whatever you like. Only I'm not sure if we have room in the garden for ten trees. It might have to be just the one.'

'I love you, Dad!'

Upstairs in my room, I send a text to Evie to tell her the fantastic news that I may be heading in the same direction at half-term. I hope Mum and Dad decide to go to the same resort as Evie and her family. That would be so cool!

After checking that my school bag is packed ready for the morning, I prepare for bed. I like to read in bed, and particularly enjoy browsing through *Green Teen* magazine, which is packed full of fascinating articles about the planet and what can be done to help save it. The magazine now has an Eco-info box on every page with an eco-fact in it. As I drift off to sleep, my mind swims hazily in a calm blue sea off a golden coast . . . Dodo is performing on a stage on the beach . . . Evie is with me . . . We have turned into mermaids . . . *Green Teen* magazine slips from my hand on to the bedroom floor . . .

Eco-info

Carbon emissions into the upper atmosphere are three times more damaging than at ground level. Because of this, one short-haul flight contributes as much to the greenhouse effect as running a small car for three months.

CHAPTER TWO

'I'm sooo happy you're coming on holiday, too, Lola!' Evie exclaims, giving me a hug. 'I really hope your mum and dad decide to come to the same resort!'

We are sitting in the dappled shade of the school tree, waiting for the first bell. Shrubberylands Comprehensive has only one proper tree, which stands in a tired circle of earth in the middle of the main courtyard, and there is a circular bench around its greyish trunk. Some people used to scratch their initials into the bark until the whole school was threatened with being thrown into the school dungeons if anyone dared to deface the tree again.

'There should be more trees,' Evie remarks. 'It's sad that the school has only one.'

I nod in agreement. The scruffy bushes and thorny shrubs which line the paths between the various school buildings can hardly be called trees.

'It would be nice if the school looked more like a park and less like a big redbrick prison,' I muse. 'Couldn't they at least grow climbing roses up that awful wire mesh that fences us in? Wouldn't that look pretty?'

Evie shakes her head. 'No one cares enough,' she says. 'The place is a dump.'

Amelia swans past with her best friend, Jemima, followed by an eager gaggle of giggling hangers-on.

'It's pathetic!' I hiss. 'They all want to be Amelia's friend just because she's been bragging that her family knows some stupid celebrities!'

I don't know if she hears me say this, but she turns in our direction and, curling her upper lip slightly, lets an empty crisp packet drop to the ground.

Evie immediately leaps across the courtyard, picks up the crisp packet and says, 'There's a bin over there, Amelia. Go and put your rubbish in it.'

Amelia's eyes have narrowed to slits as I walk over to Evie. She gives us a look which is obviously meant to shrivel us on the spot. 'Go and put it in

11

the bin yourselves, you remnants!' she snaps, spitting like an angry cobra. 'Me and the So Cool Girls don't do dirty work, do we?'

'No way, Amelia!' Jemima and the other girls chorus, obediently. Three of our friends—Cassia, Ellen and Salma—have seen what is happening and come to stand beside us, lending us their support.

Amelia tosses her long blond hair contemptuously and, with a little swagger, wanders slowly away, followed by the so-called So Cool Girls, who keep throwing us stupid backwards glances, grinning and whispering to each other.

'Why did she call us remnants?' I ask, puzzled.

'She means we're like the leftovers that no one else wants,' Evie explains. 'You know what Amelia's like. If you're someone she doesn't rate, you're nothing—you're lower than an earthworm.'

Cassia, Ellen and Salma nod in agreement.

'And she's meaner than a hyena!'

Cassia says, angrily. 'I don't know why all those girls want to hang around with her!'

'Because they're all airheads, that's why,' Evie replies. 'If you sent them all for a brain scan, you wouldn't find any brain. That's why they hang around in a gang to make themselves look big— because they're associating with the biggest airhead of all! And Amelia has to be the centre of attention, of course.'

'I don't like gangs,' I remark. 'Gangs make people stupid. They make people do things they don't want to do. They make them all follow the leader, like stupid sheep.'

'We're not a gang, are we?' says Ellen. 'We're just friends. I would never suck up to someone just to impress them!'

'I prefer sheep to Amelia,' Evie comments. 'But she's given me an idea . . .'

*   *   *

'So tell me about your idea,' I say to

13

Evie at morning break, since our earlier conversation was interrupted by some lessons. We are back under the school tree.

'I think we should greenify the school! Clean it up and green it up! When I saw Amelia drop that crisp packet, I really saw red. And then I saw green. If you see what I mean.'

'I think so . . .'

'There are so many stupid wasteful things going on here—people dropping litter, leaving lights on, wasting water, piling up rubbish instead of recycling, wasting paper—can you think of anything that's green at this school?'

'The uniform?'

'That doesn't count. It's a yucky slime-green, anyway. No one in their right mind wears slime-green, except at Shrubberylands Comprehensive.'

'Some of the food in the canteen is green.'

'If you're referring to the mouldy sandwich I had at the end of last term, that is definitely the wrong sort of green!' Evie pulls down the corners of her mouth and makes a gagging sound.

'Pleeurgh!'

'You're right, though,' I say. 'There's certainly room for improvement around here—it would be a challenge.'

'It might even be the eco-worriers' biggest challenge ever!' Evie pronounces. 'So what are we waiting for? Let's start the war on waste. We can start by not wasting time!'

'Great!' I agree. 'But where do we start?'

We look at each other doubtfully. Then Evie's green eyes light up. 'I know!' she exclaims. 'We need a teacher to help get things going. And I know which teacher to ask . . .'

'Mr Woodsage!' we shout in unison.

'You called,' says a voice, making us both jump.

Mr Woodsage appears from round the other side of the school tree where he has apparently been sitting, eating a banana. He is a tall, thin man with little round glasses and short, stubbly hair and a beard.

'I couldn't help overhearing your conversation,' he says. 'And I think it's a great idea. This school could definitely benefit from going green.'

Evie and I are both taken aback by Mr Woodsage's sudden appearance, but pleased by his reaction. He is the most eco-minded teacher at school, and is also one of the most popular teachers, managing to make geography fun and interesting. We particularly enjoyed his lessons on climate change last term.

'Since I know how concerned you are about the environment, I wonder if you'd be interested in helping to raise money for a charity I'm involved with. It's called Tree-aid, and it aims to stop the destruction of tropical rainforests and encourage reforestation in Africa and South America. Did you know that tropical rainforests produce forty per cent of the earth's oxygen? But people are destroying rainforests at a terrifying rate—an area the size of a football pitch disappears every minute through logging, farming, prospecting for oil and other human activities. It's vital that we stop this destruction, otherwise the trees and all the creatures which depend on them will die. And if the trees aren't there to absorb carbon dioxide from the atmosphere, global warming will get much, much worse!'

Evie and I exchange horrified looks. We have already heard about the rainforests, how important they are, and how they are under threat—but Mr Woodsage has brought home to us the fact that, as committed eco-worriers, we really should be doing something about it.

'Oh!' I exclaim. 'There are so many beautiful birds in the rainforest. I can't bear to think of them losing their habitat. They might become extinct, and that would be awful!' I'm passionate about birds.

'What can we do, sir?' Evie asks. 'We'd really like to help.'

Mr Woodsage smiles. 'I'm glad I've got your support. I'll have a think and let you know what we can do for Tree-aid. In the meantime, perhaps you'd like to have a brainstorming session about ways to make the school greener. Write down your ideas, and I'll arrange a meeting with Mrs Balderdash to discuss how to translate your ideas into positive action.' Mrs Balderdash is the head teacher at Shrubberylands Comprehensive.

'Thank you, sir!' we exclaim together.

'Don't mention it,' says Mr Woodsage. 'I'm sure we'll make a good team, and hopefully we can get lots of people involved in your Clean Up and Green Up campaign—maybe even the whole school! And if you have any good ideas for helping Tree-aid, write those down as well,' he adds. 'I suppose you could call Tree-aid a "chari-tree"!'

'Very funny, sir!' OK, so it isn't the funniest joke ever, but Evie and I are thrilled to have Mr Woodsage's support, and I am determined to think of a way to help save the rainforest, as well as greenifying the school.

The bell goes and, with a cheery wave, Mr Woodsage wanders off to the next lesson, leaving Evie and me full of eco-worrier excitement and determination, tinged with a feeling of, 'Help! What do we do NOW?'

Liam walks past at a slight distance

18

with his group of Sixth-Form friends. Liam and Evie ignore each other at school. I am used to this now, although I have to suppress a strange urge to wave wildly at Liam and call out, 'Hi, Liam! It's me—Lola!' or even worse, rush up and hug him in front of his friends. I am terrified by the possibility that one day I will lose all control and actually do this, after which I will be a social reject and no one, especially Liam, will ever talk to me again.

'Er, hello? Lola? Are you OK? You've got a strange expression on your face.' Evie is peering at me closely.

'Oh, I'm fine! Stop staring at me! We need to get to the next lesson.'

Eco-info

Rainforests are often regarded as valuable only because of the timber they provide. However, many experts believe that harvesting natural produce from the rainforests, such as fruits, nuts and oil-producing and medicinal plants, would be worth more than the timber, and wouldn't destroy the trees.

CHAPTER THREE

Evie and I are sitting on Evie's bed, frowning, chewing the ends of our felt tips and surrounded by sheets of paper, some of it screwed up into balls which we occasionally throw at each other. We are brainstorming.

'I wouldn't call this brainstorming,' says Evie, moodily. 'I'd say it's more like braindrizzling.'

'We've had some ideas,' I say, attempting to lighten the mood. 'Pass me the latest list.'

Evie chucks a piece of paper across to me. I look at it and read aloud:

'1) I can feel a spot about to erupt in the middle of my forehead. It will look like I've got a foul and yucky third eye.

'2) Ben in Year Ten doesn't know I exist . . .'

Evie snatches the piece of paper out of my hands. 'That's the wrong list!' she snaps. 'That's my List of Things to Worry About!'

'But Evie!' I exclaim. 'You've never

mentioned Ben in Year Ten. Why does it matter if he doesn't know you exist? There are loads of people who don't know you exist.'

'I KNOW! That's why I've made a List of More Important Things to Worry About. So please—can we just drop the subject of Ben in Year Ten?'

'OK! Fine with me. I will find out though . . .'

'Lola—shut up.'

I roll over on the bed.

'Get up, Lola!' Evie shouts, pushing me. 'You've just rolled on our list.' She is getting seriously stressed. Her hormones are obviously raging as she is nearly a teenager. I overheard her mum talking to my mum about 'raging hormones'. My thirteenth birthday is at half-term, so I should be celebrating becoming a teenager somewhere warm and sunny! I will be a teenager *first*—before Evie, whose birthday is in January.

Evie retrieves the now crumpled piece of paper on which we have listed our ideas for creating a cleaner and greener school environment. She

21

smooths it out, and reads:

'1) Stop wasting paper. STOP USING SUCH BIG WRITING! Ha ha! That's a joke! Look at all the paper we've just wasted making lists.'

'But it's OK,' I protest. 'We're using a pad of recycled paper made from post-consumer waste, whatever that means.'

'It means it's made from recycled toilet paper, probably,' says Evie. I drop the list, and pick it up again, gingerly.

'Does the school use only recycled paper?' Evie asks.

'I think so. But we'd better make sure because everyone gets through great wodges of the stuff every single day. We need to make sure it comes from sustainable sources at the very least. What's next on the list?'

Evie reads aloud:

'2) Put hippos in the school loo cisterns. We can make them out of cut-off plastic bottles. The hippo is submerged in the cistern so when you flush the loo, water stays in the hippo and so less is needed to fill up the cistern. This saves money when you flush the loo, and saves the school money. So you will be flushed with success! Ha ha!'

'Yes. Hilarious. What's next?'

'3) Introduce recycling bins for paper, plastic, clothing, etc.'

'Boys to have separate bin for stinking socks, I hope,' I say.

'4) Plant trees everywhere. But not on the sports fields. Obviously.

'5) Have a green canteen. Use locally-sourced fresh food and ingredients. Healthier for you and healthier for the planet. Compost all the leftovers in a school compost heap.

'6) Solar-powered eco-vending machines.

'7) Stick SWITCH ME OFF stickers above light switches and appliances often left on standby.'

'I think that's quite a good list!' I exclaim. 'Mrs Balderdash should be impressed.'

Evie looks thoughtful. 'It's OK,' she agrees. 'But we haven't really thought of anything that's going to excite people and get them involved. We don't want people to think it's boring being green, and we haven't thought of a way of raising money for Mr Woodsage's tree charity. I can't bear the thought of all those birds and animals which live in the trees, dying. We must think of something! Lola—what are you doing?'

'I'm dance-ercising! All this sitting around and thinking is making my muscles seize up, as well as my brain. And I need to stay in shape for the next Olympics.' I am going for gold in swimming and athletics.

'Of course,' says Evie. 'You're an Olympic hopeful—and I'm an Olympic hopeless! At least let me put on some music for you to dance to, otherwise you look a bit mad, randomly gyrating round the room in total silence.'

Evie has some small speakers for her iPod, and puts on 'Running on Water', which is the latest single by our new favourite band, Boys Next Door.

Evie watches me dance-ercising for a few minutes before suddenly leaping to her feet and shouting, 'YESS!'

'What?' I shout back.

'You've just given me the best idea!' she exclaims, dance-ercising with me, her red curls bouncing up and down. Her eyes are shining again.

Evie pulls off her school blouse and changes into an organic cotton T-shirt from her mum's boutique, Fashion Passion, which stocks ethical clothes. Evie's T-shirt bears the slogan *Love, Peace and Harmony* and, in smaller letters, *Be Kind to Our Earth—Good Planets Are Hard to Find.*

'What's your idea?' I ask, breathlessly. 'Stop dance-ercising for a moment, and tell me.'

'A talent show!' she exclaims. 'A talent show in aid of Mr Woodsage's charity! And to raise awareness of green issues and promote our ideas for greenifying the school. It would get loads of people involved—people love to sing and dance and do stuff. It would give them a chance to show off their talents. I'll get Liam to give me extra guitar lessons and I could play something—I'm getting quite good now. It would be such fun to put on a show. It can't fail!'

25

'Cool!' I enthuse. 'It sounds good. Exciting and entertaining!'

'Entertaining . . .' Evie repeats. 'That's it! Lola, you've just given me another great idea!'

'Amazing—I don't know how I do it!' I am pleased to be such a fount of inspiration, although I am beginning to wish I could have a few ideas myself. 'So, what is it?'

'We could call ourselves the GREEN-tertainers!'

'Brilliant! I like it!' Suddenly I have an idea—this is a relief. 'We could call the show "Let Me GREEN-tertain You".'

'Lola! That's inspired! I can't wait to tell Mr Woodsage!'

'Neither can I. This is going to be so amazing!'

*   *   *

We are both in high spirits for the rest of the evening, although we make the mistake of telling Evie's parents about our plans for the talent show. This starts them reminiscing about their own school days and how they took part in school plays and concerts. Evie's mum does some Spanish flamenco dancing with lots of foot stomping, clicking her fingers, flicking up her skirt and shouting, *'Olé!'* which is rather alarming and embarrassing.

'She'd better not do that when we're on holiday,' Evie whispers to me.

But when her dad starts to sing 'Yellow Submarine' by the Beatles, we flee upstairs to the safety of Evie's room.

'Sorry about that,' she apologises, turning up the volume on 'Running on Water' to drown out her dad's singing.

'It's OK,' I say. 'I've got parents too.'

Liam puts his head round the door and asks us to turn the volume down as he is trying to study.

We tell him about Tree-aid and our idea for a concert, and Evie asks him if he will give her extra coaching on the electric guitar, and if he'd like to take part himself.

He shakes his head. 'Sorry,' he says. 'I really like Geoff Woodsage—he's cool. But I don't want my mates thinking I'm turning into some sort of hippie tree-hugger, so you're going to have to leave me out of this. Not everyone wants to be as green as the Incredible Hulk or Shrek, you know. This sort of thing is probably for your Year anyway—I've got a lot of studying to do.'

'But you'll give me extra guitar lessons, won't you?' Evie calls after him desperately as he leaves. He doesn't answer.

'OK,' says Evie, with a sigh, 'so my family is hopeless. But I still think I deserve a handful of green stars for coming up with all these green ideas.'

'They were my ideas as well—some of them,' I point out.

'I know. These stars are for both of us.' Evie sticks some green stars to the pull-out Eco-Wallchart from *Green Teen* magazine which is pinned to the noticeboard in her room. She awards herself little green stars for every eco-friendly thing she does, and little black footprints for anything eco-unfriendly. 'Eco-worriers will triumph and turn the school green!' she exclaims.

Soon afterwards I have to go home and do my homework. But I am actually looking forward to school tomorrow. I hope Mr Woodsage likes our ideas . . .

Eco-info

Trees are known as earth's 'lungs'—they 'breathe' in harmful CO_2 and 'breathe' out the oxygen we need to survive. In fact, more than 20% of the world's oxygen is produced in the Amazon rainforest. Cutting down the trees means that less carbon dioxide is absorbed, and less oxygen is produced. What's worse, if the trees are burned (e.g. to clear forest land for grazing), they release lots of CO_2.

CHAPTER FOUR

'I don't believe it!' groans Evie, running her hands through her curls in despair. 'I just don't believe it!'

We are slumped on the seat under the school tree, reeling from the shock which we have just received. When we went to find Mr Woodsage to tell him about our idea, we were informed by Miss Peabody, another geography teacher, that Mr Woodsage is unlikely to be back at school for a long time— possibly not until the end of term— because he has had an accident. Apparently he fell off his roof while checking his wind turbine, and has broken both legs, sprained his wrist and is wearing a neck brace.

'Poor Mr Woodsage!' I exclaim. 'He must be in so much pain. Let's make a card and get people to sign it. Miss Peabody would probably pass it on to him.'

'That's a good idea. But I can think of something even better that we could do for him,' says Evie, a determined look on her face.

'What's that?'

'We should go ahead and do this concert for Tree-aid, and make him really proud when he hears about it. He might even be well enough to come to it.'

'That's a really great idea.'

'So why are you looking like a frightened ferret about to walk a tightrope?'

'Frightened ferret?' I exclaim, indignantly. 'I'm not frightened. And I'm nothing like a ferret.'

'It was just an expression. I'm wondering why you don't seem very enthusiastic about the concert.'

'I am enthusiastic. I'm just concerned that the whole thing is going to be a lot more difficult without Mr Woodsage's support.'

Evie still looks determined. 'It may be more difficult,' she concedes. 'But we've got to try. Have you got that list of ideas for the Clean Up and Green Up campaign?'

'Yes.'

'So what are we waiting for? Come on!'

'Where are we going?' I ask.

'To see Mrs Balderdash!'

'But . . . but . . .' I have to run to keep up with Evie. I admire her determination, and I certainly want the campaign and the concert to happen— but I have always found Mrs Balderdash worrying.

*   *   *

'Come in!' barks a deep, husky voice. Mrs Balderdash is sitting behind a huge, highly polished wooden desk. She is almost as wide as the desk and is wearing an alarming tweed suit buttoned tightly across her chest. 'Speak!' she orders.

I open my mouth but no words come out.

Evie grabs the list from me and thrusts it at Mrs Balderdash. 'We think the school needs to go green and these are some of our ideas,' she says, gabbling slightly. 'And Mr Woodsage wanted us to raise money for Tree-aid and we want to put on a talent show to raise money and awareness for Mr Woodsage—I mean, for Tree-aid. But also for Mr Woodsage. To make him feel better,' she ends, lamely.

Mrs Balderdash perches a pair of pince-nez glasses on her beaky nose and considers our list. 'So you are seeking my permission?' she asks.

'Er, yes.'

'I see no reason why not. I know all about Tree-aid. Mr Woodsage has talked to me about it before. I agree that it would be an excellent idea to stage this concert. It would have the additional benefit of cheering up Mr Woodsage. So go ahead!' she booms. 'I shall put Miss Peabody in charge of helping you to organise it.'

'Oh—thank you!' we chorus.

'As for your suggestions for making the school a cleaner, greener place, you will no doubt be pleased to hear that I have already arranged for solar panels to be installed very soon, and we shall be installing recycling bins in the main courtyard. All of the school's stationery and toilet paper is made from recycled material. I shall discuss your other suggestions in due course, but you have my permission to go ahead and pick up litter, switch off lights that are left on unnecessarily, and, with the school caretaker's permission and help, you may put hippos in the loos. I also think that it is a splendid idea to have a school compost heap, and I shall discuss it with the kitchen staff. In the meantime, good luck to you!'

Evie and I leave the head teacher's office feeling slightly dazed.

'Mrs Balderdash is quite . . .' I begin.

'Large?' says Evie.

'Yes. But she's also . . .'

'Nice?'

'Yes. And she's . . .'

'Green?'

'Yes. All of the above! She's cool! Shrubberylands Comprehensive isn't exactly a state-of-the-art zero-carbon school—yet. But it seems to be heading that way. It's up to us to help it along.' I now see Mrs Balderdash in a completely different light. And I am feeling much more hopeful about the talent show.

*   *   *

At the end of morning lessons, Evie and I slip out into the main corridor which is full of bodies all bumping and jostling, and everyone is shouting at the top of their voices. One of the teachers appears at a classroom door and bawls, 'Stop that confounded racket!' Miss Peabody also appears, opening and closing her mouth. But no one can hear her and everyone ignores her. Amelia and her So Cool Girls barge into us from behind, and Amelia sweeps past, catching my glasses, which I have put on to read my new timetable, with her elbow. I feel tears spring into my eyes as I scrabble on the floor to retrieve my glasses and save them from stampeding feet.

'Oh, dear! How clumsy of me! I DO apologise,' Amelia calls back over her shoulder in a sarcastic voice.

Evie helps me to my feet and we take refuge in the library, also known as the Resource Centre, which is a place guaranteed to be Amelia-free as she considers it an uncool place to be.

The library has more people using computers than reading books. We find Cassia, Ellen and Salma and design a Get Well card for Mr Woodsage. We also make a small poster inviting people to come for auditions for the talent show next Monday during lunch break in the drama studio. We have already gained Miss Peabody's permission for this. Cassia, Ellen and Salma let out small whoops of delight when we tell them about the talent show, earning a disapproving look from Miss Lovely the librarian. They ask if they can be in the show.

'We can do a gymnastics display,' enthuses Ellen. Cassia and Salma nod—they are all talented gymnasts.

'That would be great,' I say.

We run off several copies of the poster and print out the design for Mr Woodsage's card. It shows an ill-looking tree with a sad face on its trunk and a thermometer in its mouth, surrounded by a group of fluffy woodland creatures bringing gifts and flowers and looking concerned. The tree has broken one of its branches, which is in a sling.

'You don't think it's a bit . . . er . . . naff?' Evie asks as we walk down the corridor to the school noticeboard. It was mainly her idea.

'I think it's sweet,' I say. 'It's naff—but sweet as well. It's the thought that counts, as they say. We'll go to the art room and stick it on some card and get people to sign it.'

Evie pins a talent show poster on the noticeboard. We stick another poster on the board outside the drama studio, and another one outside the canteen. 'I suppose it will be mainly our Year downwards who are likely to want to be in it,' I comment, realistically. 'Older Years aren't going to want to take directions from us, are they?'

'I suppose not,' Evie agrees. 'Unless I can persuade Liam . . .' Her green eyes have a glint in them. Evie is good at persuading.

Two overweight boys from our year called Jamie and Oliver waddle out of the canteen, still stuffing their faces with chips and doughnuts.

'We have got to do something about the canteen!' Evie groans. 'There should at least be a healthy food option.'

'There is,' I remark. 'It's a lettuce leaf with a slug on it.'

'But is it an organic, locally sourced slug?' Evie wants to know. 'If it's a slug that's been flown halfway across the world, that's no good.'

I shrug. 'I don't know. But I know what would be good. We could suggest that Meltonio supplies the school with ice-cream!'

Meltonio is a friend of ours who drives a specially-adapted battery-powered van selling Meltonio's Marvellous Mouth-watering Eco-friendly Ices. He helped us when we rescued Pablo the penguin, which was the start of our adventure with the Eco Gardens this summer.

'Great idea!' Evie agrees. 'And I know he has an allotment where he grows fruit and veg. Perhaps he and some of the other allotment owners would consider selling some of their produce to the school. You can't get much more locally sourced than that.'

'Wow!' I exclaim. 'I'd say we're definitely brainstorming now.'

'We need brain food,' Evie says, and we go outside to sit under the school tree and eat our packed lunches.

'It's weird to think that only yesterday poor Mr Woodsage was sitting here eating a banana,' I observe, munching my Whole-earth organic peanut butter sandwich on whole-grain bread and waving a whole carrot around to emphasise the point. Evie has brought a tub of her dad's homemade sun-dried tomato pasta.

'Stuffing your faces?' sneers a familiar voice. Amelia and the So Cool Girls swagger past, sniggering.

'Just ignore her,' I tell Evie, feeling her bristling with anger beside me, like a cat about to spring. 'She just wants a reaction—don't give it to her.'

'You're right,' says Evie. 'She's not worth it. It's sad that her role models are skinny supermodels who look like stick insects, and boring celebrities.'

'Do you think she'll try to cause trouble when we're putting the talent show together?' I ask, nervously. 'She might try to wreck the auditions on Monday.'

'She can try—she won't succeed,' Evie replies, firmly.

'I'm just worried because Miss Peabody's hopeless at keeping control,' I say. 'She wouldn't say boo to a beetle.'

'Try not to worry,' Evie advises. 'If you go on finding things to worry about, I shall have to start another list.'

I grin. 'OK,' I say. 'I'll try not to worry, although we are eco-worriers!'

Eco-info

During his or her lifetime, the average person in the UK will use four thousand rolls of toilet paper. Now there's a worrying thought.

CHAPTER FIVE

The following Monday, Dad beams at me over his cornflakes. 'I've got some news about half-term,' he says.

'Yes?' I say, breathlessly, my knife poised, about to butter my toast. Is he about to tell me that we shall soon be jetting off to the same resort as Evie? Oh, please! Please make my dreams come true!

'I've booked us a holiday at the Mystic Stones eco-retreat in Cornwall,' Dad announces. 'I knew you'd be pleased,' he adds, happily surveying my fixed grin.

'That's . . . great, Dad,' I whisper, my voice strange and slightly strangled. I don't want Dad to see how disappointed I am—he evidently thinks he has booked the best holiday ever.

'There's even a wind farm next to the campsite!' Dad adds enthusiastically.

'How . . . wonderful,' I say. 'I must go—I'll be late for school.'

'But you haven't eaten your toast.'

*　　　*　　　*

'What's wrong, Lola?' Evie asks, as we walk to school.

'I just found out where we're going for our holiday,' I say, in a voice which comes out as a croak. It is a sunny morning, but I feel as though a huge cloud is hanging over me.

Evie peers at me closely. 'It's not a Sunshine Resort, is it?' she guesses, correctly.

I shake my head. 'Dad's been going on about how green he is ever since he had his van converted to run on rechargeable batteries. And now he's gone one step further along the path to green enlightenment—I think he wants to turn into a little god of greenness. So he's taking us all on a green getaway to an eco-retreat in Cornwall, right next to a wind farm.'

Evie looks startled. 'I never realised your dad was that green!' she exclaims.

'I don't think he is—really,' I say. 'I'm just so disappointed that I'm not going to be celebrating my thirteenth birthday with you, somewhere hot and sunny.' My lower lip trembles, and I quickly bite it as I don't want to seem too pathetic.

'Oh, Lola!' Evie says, giving me a hug. 'I shall miss you too—I really will! But just think how eco-friendly your holiday will be. Do you really want to be like my family, jetting off to a Sunshine Resort with all those horrid carbon emissions filling up the sky behind us?'

The answer to this is simple—it is 'yes'. I would give anything to be like Evie and her family, with all their horrid carbon emissions. But, as a committed eco-worrier, I cannot really admit to this. So I make a non-committal noise which sounds a bit like 'hrrm'. Then my voice comes out as a self-pitying bleat as I say, 'I shall be celebrating my birthday in the middle of a field, probably in a torrential downpour of rain, surrounded by sheep and cows.'

'That will be . . . nice,' says Evie. She squeezes my arm. 'We'll keep in touch,' she says. 'All through that week. Make sure your dad takes his laptop—we can email each other. But right now you need some serious cheering up. So let's look forward to lunch break and the auditions!'

We discuss how many acts we can fit into the show, which we think should last for at least an hour, maybe with a ten-minute interval. Evie thinks there should be twelve acts, but I think we could squeeze in a few more. 'We don't want to disappoint people,' I say.

'Talking about disappointing people, how do we break it to them if they're not good enough to take part?' I ask, frowning. I hate hurting people's feelings but I also want the show to be good.

'We let them down gently,' says Evie, firmly. 'Tell them not to give up, even if they didn't make it this time.'

'What if they cry?' I ask.

Evie looks exasperated. 'I don't know—we give them counselling. Or offer them a tissue.'

I try to look thoughtful. 'We need a variety of acts,' I comment. 'Not all the same. We've already got you on the guitar.'

'That's not a bad start,' says Evie, giggling excitedly. 'Let's go and find out who else wants to be in it. I hope we can fit everyone into the drama studio!'

*   *   *

When we reach the drama studio at lunchtime, Miss Peabody is the only person there, bobbing about like a nervous chicken, all twitchy head movements and fluttering hand gestures. Her mousey brown hair is piled up on top of her head in an untidy bun. She seems agitated. I feel nervous too, but am doing my best to seem cool, calm and laid-back, like Evie seems to be. We don't want to put people off.

'Er, where is everyone?' I whisper to Evie.

'I've been on the Tree-aid website,' trills Miss Peabody excitedly. 'It's really interesting. You girls should take a look!'

'We already have,' says Evie. 'We found out that one pound pays for ten trees and a hundred pounds for a thousand trees, which is enough to cover a football pitch.'

'Aha!' cries Miss Peabody shrilly. 'Excellent research. Well done, both of you!'

I look around nervously. I am worried that Miss Peabody is going to put people off. But so far no one has appeared for the auditions, despite the large *AUDITIONS—HERE!!—NOW!!!* poster which we stuck up outside the drama studio. Evie still doesn't seem too worried.

She leans out into the corridor and yells, 'Come on, people! You don't have to be on the school's Gifted and Talented Register to take part in this. You just have to want to have fun and raise money for charity.'

'Well said!' Miss Peabody squeals. Then she giggles. 'You're going to like what I'm about to tell you,' she says in a confidential whisper, leaning towards us. Evie backs away slightly. 'I've been in touch with the organisers of Tree-aid and told them what we're doing. And guess what? They're going to send us special Tree-aid collecting boxes and stickers, AND a thousand *Make Deforestation History* wristbands, manufactured from sustainably-tapped natural rubber! Isn't that COOL?'

'A thousand wristbands . . .'echoes Evie. I know what she is thinking—that is quite a lot of wristbands. So far, not a single person has turned up to audition and I am beginning to get an uncomfortable feeling in my stomach. Evie is starting to look nervous. What if this talent show never happens? What are we going to do with a thousand wristbands? I don't want to let Mr Woodsage down. And it sounds wrong when Miss Peabody says words like 'cool'.

'Er, that's great!' I say, not wishing to seem ungrateful. 'Did you give Mr Woodsage our card, Miss?'

'Oh, yes! I certainly did! He was very touched to see that almost everyone from his classes had signed it.'

Amelia and Jemima were the only two who refused to sign the card because the last time they saw Mr Woodsage he told them off for reading a shopping magazine during a lesson. They are so petty.

'This is hopeless,' Evie says, suddenly. 'No one's coming. We're going to run out of time if we don't do something. Hang on—I've got an idea.' She rummages in her school bag and produces a bar of dark, organic chocolate, which her mum says is a good source of iron, which we both need now that we are nearly teenagers with raging hormones. Brandishing the chocolate above her head she stands in the doorway of the drama studio and yells, 'Free chocolate for the first person or act to come forward and audition for the best talent show ever!'

A few minutes later the two overweight boys, Jamie and Oliver, sidle into the studio and stand awkwardly, eyeing the chocolate bar and drooling slightly.

'Welcome!' shrills Miss Peabody. 'It's good to know that you two boys care about our planet and share our concern about deforestation in Africa and South America.'

Jamie and Oliver stare at her blankly. Evie takes charge.

'So what do you do?' she asks.

Jamie and Oliver pull down the corners of their mouths and shrug their shoulders.

Evie gets impatient. 'You have to do something,' she says. 'You have to perform. Then you get the chocolate.'

Jamie and Oliver seem to understand this and start whispering together. Then they stand still, looking at us and grinning.

'OK,' says Evie. 'Go for it.'

'We do impressions,' says Jamie. He takes a deep breath and puffs out his chest and his cheeks. He looks like a puffer fish in school uniform. Oliver points a chubby finger at him and then suddenly jabs him in one cheek.

'BANG!' they both shout, making us all jump.

'He was a balloon,' Oliver explains. 'Can we have the chocolate now?'

'Is that all?' Evie says. But the boys don't reply as their mouths are full of chocolate.

I can see that Evie is about to erupt angrily, but at that moment seven giggling girls from our Year—though not from our class—spill into the room. I recognise them as Skye, Megan, Tegan, Karlie, Chelsey, Yasmin and Aisha.

'What went bang?' asks Skye.

'He did,' Evie replies wearily, jerking her head at Jamie. 'Have you come to audition?'

'Ohmigod—no! Have we? I mean—like—what? We just came to see what went bang. I don't know if we're auditioning! Ohmigod! Audition?' They all start giggling and chattering together, like a little flock of parakeets.

'FOR GOODNESS' SAKE, MAKE UP YOUR MINDS! HAVE YOU COME TO AUDITION OR HAVEN'T YOU?' Evie's hormones have obviously hit boiling point and she is becoming seriously stressed. Her face is flushed pink beneath her freckles.

The girls stand in shocked silence, staring at Evie with open mouths.

Miss Peabody clears her throat

50

nervously. 'We're trying to put a show together, girls,' she begins, tentatively. 'It's to raise money for Tree-aid, and it's meant to cheer up Mr Woodsage. I haven't told him about it yet—I think it should be a surprise,' she adds. 'So we'd be really grateful if you girls could think of an act and take part. It should be a lot of fun!'

The girls look at each other doubtfully. One of them, Aisha, who seems quieter and more sensible than the others, steps forward and says, 'We all go to dance class together. Perhaps we could think of a dance routine. But I don't know if we're good enough.'

'Oh, don't worry!' I exclaim. 'It's not like a competition—this is just for fun. The more people we can get to join in the better. So just tell yourselves you can do it—suspend the inner critic. We won't be judging you—at least, not too much! I'm sure you'll pass the audition,' I add, encouragingly. I'm not sure if my motivational speech has worked—the girls still look nervous— but they agree to give it a go.

'Perfect!' trills Miss Peabody. 'I'll

51

add your names to the list.' I didn't realise there was a list yet, but it sounds good. Miss Peabody is cleverer than I thought.

Other people are beginning to filter into the drama studio. We are so relieved to see Cassia, Ellen and Salma and some of our other friends who have come to lend their support. A popular boy called Jack offers to write a rap about deforestation in Africa. I know that he is good at poetry and creative writing so we add his name to the list. The fact that Jack is on the list should also encourage other people to join in. I just have to swallow my annoyance that Jack seems already to have assumed that he is to be the star of the show, and is lolling across three chairs in a corner of the drama studio, wearing a pair of dark glasses, despite the fact that all the curtains are drawn, looking cool and superior.

'Any moment now he's going to offer to sign autographs,' I hiss at Evie.

Fortunately Cassia, Ellen and Salma grab some mats and perform a sequence of handstands, forward rolls and cartwheels which distracts people's attention away from Jack.

'That was great,' I exclaim, rushing over to them and giving them all big hugs. 'You're definitely in.'

A boy called Cam is doing an impression of an eco-Dalek, walking around the studio with one arm outstretched, shouting, 'I will carbon-neutralise you!' in a staccato voice. I put him down as a 'maybe'. Evie puts him down as a 'maybe not'.

But we are both enthusiastic about a girl called Shaheen Khan, who does some beautiful Indian dancing with amazingly intricate finger and eye movements. She tells us that she will wear Indian clothes to dance in, and bring in some real Indian music. Her uncle, who is a musician, might even bring in his sitar. We put her down as a 'definitely'.

Three girls—Gemma, Victoria and Dannii—offer to sing. They call themselves Girls United and, with Miss Peabody accompanying them on an electric keyboard which she has found in a corner of the studio—Miss

53

Peabody has many hidden talents, I have decided—they manage to sing a whole song, 'Loving You to Bits' by the Honeybabes, completely out of tune. They sound like the neighbourhood feline population caterwauling in the dead of night. Jack has covered his ears with his hands, and is rocking to and fro in apparent pain.

'OK, girls,' says Miss Peabody brightly. 'We need to work on that!'

'Do we let them down now or later?' I whisper to Evie.

'Er, let's give them a chance,' Evie whispers back. She seems to have gone off the idea of letting people down gently, or otherwise. 'Perhaps they'll get their act together. Right now we just need enough acts to fill an hour.'

A small, serious boy called Harry who wears round, black-framed glasses and spends most of his time in the library, says that he can do magic tricks.

'You'll need some serious magic to turn this load of cow poo into a show,' sneers a familiar voice. Amelia and Jemima are standing in the doorway, smirking.

To my surprise, little Harry walks over to her, reaches up and appears to fish something out from behind her right ear.

'Er, gerroff, squirt!' she exclaims. The expression on her face swiftly changes to one of complete horror as she sees what Harry is holding in his hand—a big hairy black spider! With a shrill shriek, Amelia turns and flees, followed by Jemima.

'Hooray for Harry!' I shout, and everyone cheers and claps.

'You're definitely in, Harry!' says Evie. 'Just tell me it's not a real spider.'

Harry laughs, and stuffs the toy spider in his pocket. When the excitement and hubbub has died down, a boy called Lee comes forward and offers to tell eco-jokes.

'Do you know any?' Evie asks. 'Give us an example.'

'Er, can you give me a day or two?' Lee asks.

'That wasn't very funny!' Jack calls out.

'It wasn't a joke, idiot!' Lee replies.

'I'm just asking for a bit of time to work on my act.'

'That's probably a good idea,' says Miss Peabody, who has been flitting around the studio writing down everyone's names and what they are intending to do. 'We could all do with some time to work on our acts! Might I suggest we all meet here again at lunchtime on Thursday to start rehearsing?'

'I have orchestra during lunch-break on Thursday, Miss,' says Harry, who plays the flute.

'So do I,' someone else calls out.

'And I have football practice,' says the eco-Dalek.

Eventually everyone agrees to meet back at the drama studio on Friday during lunch-break.

'Thank you all for coming!' Evie calls out as the bell rings and people start to leave. 'You've all passed the auditions! You are the Green-tertainers!'

'Will there be more free chocolate?' Jamie asks.

'No,' replies Evie, shortly.

*   *   *

Later in the afternoon, just as we are leaving the school grounds, excitedly discussing the fact that we now have singing—if you can call the out-of-tune caterwauling singing—dance, gymnastics, magic and Evie on guitar (which is nearly enough for a show but not quite), a small, thin, ginger-haired boy rushes up to us.

'I'm Harry's friend!' he says breathlessly. 'My name's Eddie. Harry told me about your talent show. It sounds great! Can I be in it?'

'I don't know,' I reply. 'It depends what you can do.'

'I can't do much,' says Eddie. 'But I've got a performing parrot. He's called Rico, and he's an African Grey. They're really intelligent, and Rico's super-intelligent. He can count! He rings a little bell, and if you say any number to him up to nineteen he'll do that exact number of rings on his bell. And I've got a skateboarding tree frog called Norman.'

57

'OK,' says Evie. 'I wasn't sure at first but the skateboarding tree frog just clinched it. Is there any way you can bring them in to show us?'

'Yes, sure! I'm friends with Mr Bunsen the biology teacher, and he'll look after Rico and Norman in the biology lab while I'm in lessons. I can bring them along on Friday, if you like.'

'Yes, please do. I've never seen a skateboarding tree frog before.'

'This is mad!' says Evie, shaking her head and laughing as we walk slowly home. 'I thought the whole thing was going to be a disaster at first, especially when no one showed up. But, with a lot of hard work, we might be able to put together a show to make Mr Woodsage proud.'

I nod agreement. 'Eddie's given me an idea,' I say. 'Since he's bringing in his parrot and his tree frog, do you think we could ask Kate Meadowsweet to bring in Mr Macawber?' Mr Macawber is a large blue and yellow parrot at the Eco Gardens. 'I'm sure she said that they sometimes take some of the creatures from the Eco Gardens into schools to show how amazing they are and what a tragedy it is that the rainforest where they live is being destroyed. It might bring home to people how all those animals and beautiful birds depend on the trees they live in for their survival.'

'That's a totally inspired idea!' Evie agrees enthusiastically. 'It would make people want to give even more money to Tree-aid to help protect the animals and birds who live in the trees. You're a genius, Lola!'

I smile proudly. A touch of Eco-Worrier Inspiration never goes amiss!

Eco-info

The red-eyed tree frog of the South American rainforest has special pads on its long, thin fingers and toes which produce a sticky mucus that 'glues' the frog to smooth, slippery leaves and branches. This is just one of the creatures which depends on the rainforest for its survival. If too many trees are cut down, it will become extinct.

CHAPTER SIX

I am sleeping like a log from sustainable woodland when my phone beeps, waking me up. It is only seven a.m.! I have a message from Evie: *Bring plastic bottles round to mine NOW.*

I send a message back: *2 early*!

But I know that Evie will not let me go back to sleep so, with a sigh, I get dressed and go downstairs to the kitchen where Dad is making an early morning cup of tea.

'Dad, can I take all the plastic bottles from the recycling bin?'

'Er, where do you want to take them?'

'To school. To put in the loos.'

Dad gives me a puzzled look.

'Don't ask, Dad—it's too early.'

I fill a recyclable bin liner with two-litre plastic bottles, which I take round to Evie's house along with my school bag. She opens the door and lets me in.

'I haven't even had breakfast,' I

grumble.

'We'll have some toast while we cut bottles,' she says, firmly.

We started cutting plastic bottles in half at Evie's house last night to make the hippos the right size to fit in the cisterns of the school loos to cut down on water usage, but ran out of time and bottles, so Evie suggested I bring some more bottles in the morning.

Cutting plastic bottles in half is even less fun than it sounds. Because I am not properly awake, I manage to cut my finger on a sharp plastic edge. 'Ouch!'

'No eco-gain without eco-pain,' says Evie helpfully, fetching me a plaster.

Liam comes into the kitchen to get a drink. He looks half-asleep, and his hair is tousled. I nearly cut my finger again.

'What are you two doing?' he asks, looking at the cut-up bottles curiously.

'Saving water,' Evie replies. 'Saving the planet.'

'You could dramatically cut down on water consumption by spending less time in the bathroom,' says Liam.

'You're always in there—I can never get in. Think of all the dried-up lakes that might fill up again if you stopped washing your hair ten times a day.'

'I don't wash my hair ten times a day!' Evie retorts. 'And I wish you'd stop drinking that imported orange juice. Think of all the air miles it has to travel, and now you're eating an imported banana!'

'So what?' mumbles Liam through a mouthful of banana. 'What would happen to all the developing world banana growers if we stopped importing their bananas? They'd lose their business and starve! Do you want that to happen, just so that you can save on air miles?'

Evie looks confused. She frowns. 'When can I have a guitar lesson?' she asks, changing the subject.

'I don't know,' says Liam, unhelpfully. 'Have a banana.' And he leaves the room.

*　　　*　　　*

Mr Keys, the caretaker, has

thoughtfully provided us with rubber gloves to wear while we put the hippos in the cisterns. We are going to put them in the girls' loos and Mr Keys has agreed to put them in the boys' loos.

'This is NOT my idea of fun!' I mutter, as I start putting hippos in cisterns.

A lot of people ask us what we are doing. They seem quite interested when we explain. Unfortunately, Amelia and the So Cool Girls are hanging around, as they often do, adjusting their hair in the mirrors.

'Doing your work experience, are you?' Amelia snarls at me to a ripple of delighted tittering from the So Cool Girls. 'Practising for your future career as a loo attendant?'

'Someone has to do it, Amelia,' I reply, coolly. 'If you really want to know, we're waging war on waste, which includes wasting water. This is part of our Clean Up and Green Up campaign.'

'Whatever,' says Amelia, sounding bored. 'Some of us have a life!' She drifts out of the girls' loos, followed by her devoted gang of So Cool Girls, all of them giggling and jeering at us.

'Thank goodness they've gone!' I say. 'Have you got one of those stickers before we leave?'

Evie presses a SWITCH ME OFF sticker on to the wall, just above the light switch. We printed them out in the Resource Centre yesterday with the help of Miss Lovely.

A girl walks past and is about to drop an apple core into the rubbish bin when Evie says, 'You should put that on the school compost heap! It will rot down.'

'Rot down yourself!' the girl retorts rudely, dropping the apple core in the bin and pushing past us.

'How rude!' Evie exclaims. 'What's your problem?' she yells after the girl, who ignores us and walks away down the corridor.

'Oh, I know who she is,' I say. 'Her name's Kelsey and she wants to be in Amelia's gang, but Amelia keeps snubbing her. I don't know why.'

'Well there's no need to take it out on us,' Evie says. 'It's going to be hard work persuading people like that to go green,' she adds, with a sigh.

*   *   *

We are still wearing our rubber gloves, waiting outside the boys' loos with a black bin liner half-full of spare hippos waiting for Mr Keys to emerge so that we can give him more of the hippos, if he needs them.

Instead of Mr Keys, Liam and his friends come through the door. Liam tries to ignore us, but his friends start grinning. 'Hey, Liam! Your little sister and her friend are hanging around outside the boys' loos wearing rubber gloves. Is that weird, or what?'

'Don't ask me,' Liam mutters, hurrying away.

I feel myself turning red, but Evie just looks annoyed.

'Please remember to turn off lights that aren't on for a reason,' she calls after Liam and his friends. 'And turn off taps as well. You always leave them running, Liam. Remember that flushing the loo uses a lot of water. So if it's yellow, let it mellow. If it's brown, flush it down!'

I start giggling. 'I can't believe you just said that!' I whisper.

'Who are you—my mother?' says a grumpy voice, and a boy who has just emerged from the boys' loos walks past, glaring back at us over his shoulder.

I notice that Evie is standing motionless, a strange expression on her face.

'That was Ben from Year Ten, wasn't it?' I say, astutely.

Evie nods. She seems unable to speak or move.

'Never mind—just remember your List of More Important Things to Worry About,' I say reassuringly, taking her by the arm and guiding her gently away from the boys' toilets, before she collapses from terminal embarrassment.

*   *   *

It is Friday. It is lunchtime. Miss Peabody is wearing a lime-green *Make*

Deforestation History wristband.

'Aren't these wristbands cool, girls?' she twitters.

I decide that they were cool, until Miss Peabody put one on and said it was cool! But this is mean of me. I like Miss Peabody, even if she can't keep order. Everyone in the drama studio is chattering loudly and the overexcited eco-Dalek is walking to and fro, carbon-neutralising people.

'Stop that!' says Evie, who has already been carbon-neutralised twice. 'It's getting boring. Can everyone be quiet, please? We need to get on.'

'Where's Jack?' I ask.

'He's in detention,' Lee replies. 'Jack's always in detention. I think he wants to be President of the Republic of Detention.'

'Oh, great,' says Evie. 'Let's hope he makes it to a rehearsal sometime. Have you thought of any jokes yet, Lee?'

Lee's face lights up. 'I certainly have. I've got a whole routine worked out!'

'That's excellent. Let's hear it.'

'OK.' Lee clears his throat. He clears it again. 'OK,' he says again. 'I'm nearly ready now—just need to loosen up . . .' He shakes his wrists and hands and jiggles up and down on the spot, taking deep breaths and breathing out again through his mouth in short, sharp exhalations.

Evie yawns.

'I'm ready,' says Lee. 'OK. Here goes. Why didn't the chicken cross the road?'

Everyone looks at him blankly.

'Er, because it wanted to save energy.'

Silence. Harry laughs politely. Eddie has not shown up yet. There is no sign of a parrot or a tree frog.

'Oh! I get it!' exclaims Miss Peabody. 'Because it wanted to save energy! That's very funny! Hee hee hee!' she shrieks with laughter. Evie sighs.

'Er, I've got another one,' says Lee, who looks slightly scared by Miss Peabody's reaction. 'Why didn't the chicken get out of bed in the morning?'

Another blank silence.

'Because it wanted to save energy?' Evie suggests.

'Er, yes!' says Lee, giving her the

thumbs-up.

Miss Peabody laughs again, a little less uproariously this time.

'Do all your jokes end in the punchline, "Because it wanted to save energy", Lee?' I ask.

Lee shrugs. 'I'm doing my best,' he says, defensively.

'OK—it's still early days,' says Evie, kindly. 'Perhaps you could think of a few different jokes . . .'

'Oh no,' I say. 'Here come Amelia and her cronies.'

Amelia and the So Cool Girls troop into the drama studio and flop down on some chairs at the side of the room.

'We've come to watch the freak show!' she calls out. 'Three jeers for the freaks—Hip hip, blah blah! Hip hip, blah blah!'

'Amelia!' squeaks Miss Peabody. 'That isn't very nice! I shall have to ask you to leave.' But Amelia just curls her upper lip in a slight sneer and stays where she is. 'If you won't do as you're asked, I shall have to talk to the head of Year!' says Miss Peabody, sounding upset.

'Whatever,' says Amelia.

Suddenly there is a loud whistling sound and a grey and red bird swoops into the drama studio and lands on Amelia's head. It delicately raises one leg and squirts a splodge of white poo on to her shoulder. Leaping to her feet with a piercing shriek, Amelia starts running distractedly around in circles, while the parrot takes off and flies in circles round the room above our heads, just as Eddie, clutching a skateboard, runs into the room shouting, 'Rico! Rico! Come here!' Everyone laughs excitedly as Amelia rushes from the room, followed by the Slightly Less Cool Than Usual Girls.

'Perhaps she'll give up annoying us soon,' says Evie. 'First she gets attacked by a spider, now a parrot! Hopefully she won't want to come back.'

Everyone is entranced by Rico the African Grey parrot and his ability to count, ringing his little bell the correct number of times to correspond with a given number. We tell Eddie that we have had an email from Kate

Meadowsweet at the Eco Gardens, and she has agreed to bring in Mr Macawber and a few other small rainforest creatures when we have the talent show. Eddie seems pleased, and says that it will be nice for Rico to see some friends.

I am fascinated by Norman the skateboarding tree frog, whom Eddie has produced from his shirt pocket. Norman is a big hit with everyone.

'See how he uses his sticky toes to cling on to the skateboard,' says Eddie, giving the skateboard a little push. We all watch as the tiny emerald-green frog with the bulging red eyes trundles slowly across the drama studio floor.

'Can he do any stunts?' Lee asks.

Eddie shakes his head. 'No,' he replies. 'He just likes to sit.'

Miss Peabody claps, and everyone joins in the applause. Norman the skateboarding tree frog is a hard act to follow, but Shaheen has brought in her Indian costume and her music, and we are all spellbound by her beautiful dancing.

'I had a word with Uncle,' she says

when she has finished her dance. 'He says he will bring in his sitar soon, if you wish.'

'Oh, that's very kind!' exclaims Miss Peabody. 'We would love that!'

There is just enough time left for Miss Peabody to grab her keyboard, and for Girls United to have another go at murdering 'Loving You to Bits'. This time it is not as bad as before, and they even manage to hit one or two right notes!

Skye, Megan, Tegan, Karlie, Chelsey, Yasmin and Aisha are disappointed that there isn't enough time left for them to do their dance, but Miss Peabody promises that they can be first at our next rehearsal, which is scheduled for next Monday at lunch-break.

*　　　*　　　*

'Do you really think we've seen the last of Amelia at rehearsals?' I ask, as Evie and I walk home with Ellen, who lives round the corner from us in Newton Close. We are all walking arm in arm.

'I don't know,' Evie replies. 'I certainly hope so. But you can never be sure where Amelia's concerned . . .'

'Oh, I don't want to think about Amelia.' I say. 'And I don't want to think about how I'm going to survive a week knee-deep in mud on a campsite in Cornwall. And finally I don't want to think about homework. The school could save so much paper if it stopped giving us essays to write.'

'At least you can put your essay in the recycling bin when you've finished it,' Ellen comments. 'And I've seen where they put the school compost heap behind the canteen—it stinks!'

'I'm not surprised,' says Evie. 'Some of the food in the canteen looks as though it's already been recycled—through someone's intestines!'

'EEUW!' Ellen and I exclaim together. 'GROSS!'

Eco-info

Leaving a one hundred watt light bulb on for half an hour uses enough energy to fill a party balloon with CO_2.

CHAPTER SEVEN

'You'll be pleased to hear that we won't be staying in a tent!' says Dad, beaming at me over his Saturday morning cup of tea. We have the same brown eyes, but Dad's hair is a lighter shade of brown than mine, and is receding slightly, with greyish bits around his ears. 'We'll be staying in a log cabin made entirely from sustainable timber in the Mystic Stones eco-retreat—there's even a well where we can fetch our own fresh water from the bosom of Mother Earth. That's what it says in the brochure. Even the brochure is made from recycled paper—isn't that great? I knew you'd be pleased. Why aren't you eating your toast?'

I have completely lost my appetite. All I can think of is Evie lying on a sun lounger beside a pool on a palm-fringed paradise island.

I push back my chair. 'Is it OK if I go to Evie's house?' I ask.

'Yes, love,' says Dad. 'I expect you

want to tell her all about the holiday we're going on! I hope she isn't too disappointed that she can't come with us this time. But if it's a nice place, we might go there again . . . and again . . . and again . . .'

* * *

And again . . . and again . . . and again . . . Dad's words are echoing round my brain as I flump down on the edge of Evie's bed, where she is still sprawled, having a lie-in.

'What's up, Lola?' Evie asks.

'Please PLEASE hide me in your suitcase and take me with you to the Costa Fortuna!' I plead.

'I would love to. But I can't. My suitcase is already stuffed with holiday clothes, flip-flops, suncream and swimwear. There isn't room for you. Oh, Lola! Don't look like that! I'm only teasing. I'm really going to miss you, especially on your birthday. I think we both need cheering up—let's go to the Shrubberylands Shopping Zone. Mum's got a sale on at her shop—and

75

we might see if we can find Meltonio and ask him about supplying the school with fresh organic food.'

'And have an ice-cream?'

'Oh—definitely!'

*   *   *

Evie's mum's boutique, Fashion Passion, is full of shoppers browsing through the sale rail. A lot of items are reduced, including the organic cotton *Love, Peace and Harmony* T-shirt which I really like. Evie is wearing another organic cotton T-shirt from Fashion Passion today—it is sky-blue with a rainbow-coloured butterfly on it. She has lent me a pink T-shirt with a red heart on it.

'You're like a walking advertisement for my clothes,' Evie's mum says, laughing.

'We can be your models!' Evie says, tossing her red curls and strutting up and down the shop, striking poses. The other customers turn to look at her and smile, and I can't stop giggling.

'I'm going to wear this top when I

play my guitar at the show,' says Evie, who has been practising hard in her room for the past few days. She has chosen a piece called 'Greensleeves'— appropriately. Liam told her that it wasn't meant to be played on an electric guitar, and has been teasing her about it. He had rather grudgingly offered to help her with it, but since we were found lurking outside the boys' loos wearing rubber gloves, he has been noticeably less keen to have anything to do with us.

As we leave the shop, we nearly bump into Amelia and Jemima.

'Try looking where you're going,' says Amelia, sarcastically. 'Have you just been in the hippie shop? Is that where you get all your weird hippie clothes?'

'It's not a hippie shop. It's my mum's shop.' Evie's cheeks have turned white beneath her freckles, with two angry red spots.

'I know,' sneers Amelia. 'But you've got to admit that only a sad hippie freak would wear a T-shirt which says "Love, Peace and Harmony"!'

'Just because all your clothes are produced in sweatshops by child labourers working in dreadful slum conditions for next-to-nothing so that selfish people like you can wear cheap, fashionable clothes!' Evie seethes.

'My clothes are not cheap!' Amelia retorts. 'I have taste, unlike some people! I have bags of style . . .'

'And some stylish bags,' says Jemima.

We all look at her. This is the first time that Jemima has said something faintly amusing.

'I get all my fashion tips from Jadene,' Amelia continues, ignoring Jemima. 'She's a friend of my family, you know. And she's going to model my dad's range of clothes. He's branching out into the fashion business. He's going to put your mum and her sad little shop in the shade— just you wait!' She pushes past us and struts away, swinging her hips.

'Don't take any notice of her,' I say to Evie, placing a comforting hand on her arm. I notice that her fists are clenched. 'Amelia's all talk—you should know that by now. She's an attention-seeker, and she can't handle the fact that more and more people are getting interested in our talent show, and not many people are interested in her!'

'That's true, I suppose,' says Evie. There was a lot of talk about the Green-tertainers going around the school on Friday afternoon before we came home, and several more people came forward wanting to take part, including a guitarist and several girl singers who are going to audition on Monday. Miss Peabody has suggested that we start selling wristbands next week to help spread the message about Tree-aid and the talent show.

'We've got it all to look forward to,' I say, encouragingly. 'So cheer up!'

Evie calms down and gives me a hug. We smile at each other. Soon Evie has an even bigger smile on her face as we have found Meltonio's ice-cream van parked just outside the shopping zone, and we have bought ourselves two Organic Death by Chocolate Triple Flakes.

'Mmm!' says Evie.

'Mmmmmmmm!' I say.

Meltonio likes our idea about supplying the school with ice-cream and organic fruit and veg from the allotments. His droopy black moustache ripples as his face creases into a big smile. He says that he will discuss our suggestion with the school and with his friends on the allotments. Then he has to turn his attention back to his queue of customers. As we walk away, we see Jamie and Oliver stagger past with two Quadruple Scoop Banoffee Pie Tongue-teasers with extra sprinkles.

'I don't think Meltonio should supply the school with too much ice-cream,' says Evie, doubtfully.

'Plain chocolate, strawberry and vanilla would probably be best,' I agree. 'The main thing is that it's organic.'

But I am beginning to feel very full and not quite as fit as an Olympic hopeful should be. I suggest to Evie that, instead of getting a lift, we walk back to our houses, fetch our swimming costumes and go swimming at the leisure centre. Evie agrees. She says that she wants to get in shape so that she can wear her new bikini on holiday. I wish she hadn't said this! But I force a smile.

We have a lot of fun at the leisure centre, swimming with our legs clamped together and pretending to be mermaids. Evie, who is not as good at swimming as I am, finds it hard to do this without sinking, and she gets the giggles. I do some serious lengths while she flounders around in the shallow end, and I practise my racing turns in preparation for the Olympics.

On the way home, Evie picks up an acorn and announces her intention of planting it in order to carbon-offset her holiday flight. 'I'll plant it near the other two which I planted last year,' she says. 'They've grown quite a lot this year—they've both got leaves and they're looking healthy.'

Evie suggests we have a sleepover at her house, and I go home to collect my stuff. Dad is sitting at the computer. 'Look at this!' he says, calling me over. 'It's a picture of our holiday cabin in

Cornwall. Look, it's even got solar panels on the roof!' He beams at me, and I smile back.

I suddenly feel guilty for being so ungrateful for the eco-holiday which Dad has clearly booked with me in mind. After all, it is because of me and my constant nagging that Mum and Dad have been making an effort to go green. It is time that I showed a little more appreciation. I give Dad a big hug.

'It looks great, Dad. Thanks for booking a holiday for us—I can't wait! I love you!'

*   *   *

Later on, in Evie's room, I ask Evie why Liam ignored us earlier. He has now gone out with his friends, leaving behind a strong smell of Bodyblitz bodyspray—I really like the smell!

'Oh, it's because we embarrassed him in front of his friends when we were outside the boys' loos, wearing rubber gloves,' Evie replies. 'Anyone would think we committed some sort of crime! It's a shame because I want him to help me with "Greensleeves".'

She sticks another handful of green stars on her eco-chart. 'These are for the hippos in the loos,' she says firmly. 'And for the *SWITCH ME OFF* stickers. And the school recycling bins and the compost heap. It's great that the school's recycling so much waste, although people are still throwing stuff in litter bins that could be recycled. Amelia does it deliberately, just to be annoying. She dropped a banana skin right in front of my feet yesterday, and I bet it wasn't even a Fairtrade banana! I told her to pick it up but she just laughed in that annoying way she does—like a high-pitched horse—and walked away. So Cassia picked it up and took it to the compost heap.'

'The school should start its own vegetable garden—somewhere to spread the compost and grow healthy produce,' I suggest, trying to get rid of the thought of Amelia and her annoying behaviour.

'Great idea! Let's suggest it!' Evie agreed.

'OK, although it's not really the right time of year to start growing things,' I comment.

'And we've probably got enough on our plate, with the show and turning the school green,' says Evie.

'Our "Let Me Green-tertain You" show is going to be great, isn't it?' I enthuse, as we lie on Evie's bed, eating organic chocolate.

'I think it is,' Evie agrees.

'So there isn't really much to worry about, is there?' I ask.

'Not really. I made a very short list.'

'Show me.'

Evie passes me a sheet of paper headed *Things to Worry About*. There is just one word on the sheet: *Amelia*.

Eco-info

There are lots of ways to green up your wardrobe. When shopping, try to go for eco-friendly clothes which use organic cotton (produced without pesticides) or are Fair Trade. You can even buy fleeces that have fibres made out of recycled plastic bottles! To be even greener, reuse clothes—swap them with your friends or buy them from charity shops!

CHAPTER EIGHT

'Lola! Stop! Please!'

As part of my new pre-Olympic, Get Superfit regime, I have decided to jog to school every day. It is Monday and I am getting off to a flying start. Evie is struggling to keep up, and I can hear her puffing and panting behind me.

'I can't run in these shoes,' she complains. 'Can't we walk like we usually do?'

'Sorry, I can't stop!' I call back over my shoulder. I love jogging. I am wearing my running shoes and will change into my school shoes when I get to school.

At morning break I find Evie sitting under the school tree, waiting for me.

'What took you so long?' she asks. 'I've been here for ages.'

'Oh, Miss Grizlingham kept me behind at the end of design,' I reply. Evie and I are in different groups for design. Evie does electronics and I do graphics.

'Why did she keep you behind?'

'She didn't like me desk-ercising.'

'Desk-ercising?'

'Yes. It's part of my new regime. Instead of wasting time sitting still at my desk or table, I do exercises such as raising and lowering my arms or legs or shoulders, or circling my ankles, or flexing my fingers. Miss Grizlingham didn't like it. She said I couldn't do graphics and desk-ercise at the same time.'

'She probably had a point.'

A few people are dallying near the school tree, talking excitedly about the talent show. Miss Peabody rushes over with two collecting tins and a tray of *Make Deforestation History* wristbands.

'You can start selling these now,' she says. 'The suggested price is one pound, but I think people can contribute as much or as little as they can afford. I think that would be fair, don't you?'

Amelia and Jemima come over and inspect the wristbands.

'Hmm,' says Amelia, picking one up and dropping it again in distaste. 'I don't think so. Pea-green is sooo not my colour. But I think it would suit you,' she says to Evie. 'And wristbands are so dated—did no-one tell you?'

Miss Peabody clears her throat nervously. 'I hope you'll remember what we discussed with the Year head, Amelia,' she says, squeakily. 'The important thing to remember is that the whole school is a No Put-down Zone. Treat others as you would wish to be treated yourself. You agreed to all of this during our meeting with the Year head, didn't you?'

I bet she did! I can imagine that Amelia was all nicey-nicey in front of the Year head, just to get herself off the hook. She is so two-faced.

Evie and I take our collecting tins and set off to sell wristbands. They prove very popular, despite what Amelia said, and plenty of people buy them. We reassure others, who haven't brought any money, that they will be able to buy a wristband tomorrow.

I see Liam in the distance with his friends. I want to run up to him and give him a wristband. I want to ask him if we can make deforestation history together. It seems such a shame that he is worried about being seen as a hippie tree-hugger. What's wrong with hugging trees? I wish Liam and his Sixth-Form friends would wear the wristbands. It would help to make Tree-aid doubly cool. But I can't quite pluck up the courage to approach them, especially knowing that I annoyed him by hanging around outside the boys' loos. I didn't mean to annoy him!

*   *   *

'The Jack
  Is back!'
Jack makes an entrance into the drama studio, wearing his dark glasses and clicking his fingers and pointing.
'Is that a rap?' I whisper to Evie.
'It's a very short one,' she whispers back.
We tell Jack that he will have to wait for his turn, as we have promised Skye, Megan, Tegan, Karlie, Chelsey, Yasmin and Aisha that they can do their dance

first.

'OK, girls!' trills Miss Peabody. 'I think we're all ready now. So let's see your dance!'

'We call ourselves Firedance,' announces Skye, putting on some music.

The girls, who are all wearing short red skirts, red crop-tops and red tights, move first to the right, then to the left, as loud, fast, dance music pumps into the room. Then they all move to the right again, apart from Megan who moves to the left and knocks Karlie over. Karlie gets up again and they all eye each other sideways as the dance continues. Tegan gets the giggles.

At the end of the dance they stand in a row, spin round and bend over, flicking up their skirts to reveal that each of them has a large black letter on a sheet of white paper stuck to their backside. People start laughing and Jack takes off his dark glasses, presumably to see better. The letters spell out the words *DIRE EAT*.

Miss Peabody looks puzzled. 'What is "DIRE EAT"?' she asks.

The girls all crane their necks over their shoulders to look at their backsides.

'You're in the wrong place!' hisses Megan to Tegan.

'No! You're in the wrong place!' Megan hisses back at Tegan.

After some frantic re-shuffling the girls bend over again and flick up their skirts to reveal the words *TREE AID*.

'Aha!' exclaims Miss Peabody, clapping.

Everyone cheers and a few of the boys give loud wolf whistles.

'Cheeky—but fun!' says Evie, adding Firedance to our list of acts. 'At least they're helping to get the message across about Tree-aid, which is what the show's all about. We should probably get someone to stand up and give a short talk about deforestation and Tree-aid so that people at the concert know what they're contributing to.'

'Good idea!' I agree.

The eco-Dalek seems to have found the dancing very exciting and stands in front of us, arm outstretched, repeatedly carbon-neutralising us before moving on.

'What are we going to do about him?' asks Evie, who has been staring at the eco-Dalek with a bored I-am-so-not-impressed expression on her face. 'He's so . . . immature.'

'I know,' I agree. 'But I don't want to hurt his feelings by telling him he can't be in the show. Perhaps we could give him a job showing people to their seats.'

One of the girl singers is next to audition. When she has finished, I turn to Evie and say, 'You know how a mermaid's song is meant to entrance men? I think we just heard the opposite of that.'

'It was a bit of a screech, wasn't it?' Evie agrees.

Fortunately, the other girl singer is better, and Cassia, Ellen and Salma are amazing, performing cartwheels and flips from one end of the drama studio to the other. They have obviously been working hard at their routine. I feel glad that Evie and I have really good friends who we can rely on.

Then Harry does some more magic tricks. He has a magician's top hat and a magic wand, and he turns the top hat over to show us that it is empty, and taps it with his magic wand.

Jack yawns loudly. 'Get on with it!' he calls out. 'Show us the rabbit!'

'Sssh!' Miss Peabody shushes him, holding a skinny finger to her lips.

But instead of a rabbit, Harry reaches into the hat and produces Norman the skateboarding tree frog to tumultuous applause. Harry hands Norman carefully to Eddie, and people crowd round to have a closer look at the tiny frog.

Flushed with success, Harry announces: 'I will now make Jack disappear!' He goes to stand in front of Jack and says, in a loud voice: 'Jack, you've got to have extra maths lessons with Mr Grimshaw every day for the next fortnight!'

'Aaargh!' shouts Jack in a strangled voice—and he leaps up and runs from the room.

'There!' says Harry triumphantly. 'I made Jack disappear!'

Everyone laughs, and Harry takes a bow. Jack comes back into the room, grinning. I decide that he is not too bad, even if he is big-headed.

'Can I do my rap now?' he asks.

'Carry on,' says Miss Peabody.

Jack puts on some hip-hop music and his dark glasses and starts doing some street dance. Then he starts rapping:

'Now I'm no fool
I'm Mr Cool
Yes I'm the man
With the plan
To save the planet
Which is crucial—innit?
So listen to me
And plant that tree
And you will see
It will set you free
Stop global warming!
Ain't no word that rhymes with warming
Apart from swarming
Which don't fit
And this is it
So I'm telling you straight
This is your fate

It's in your hands
Wear your wristbands!'
Jack punches the air to a huge round of applause and Megan and Tegan start screaming, 'We love Jack!'

'That was pretty good,' I say to Evie. 'Although I could do without the screaming fans—it'll only make him even more big-headed.'

As a complete contrast, a tall thin boy with dark curly hair steps forward and recites Shakespeare:

'To be, or not to be: that is the question:
Whether 'tis nobler in the mind to suffer
The slings and arrows of outrageous fortune,
Or to take arms against a sea of troubles,
And by opposing end them.'

Unfortunately Amelia has chosen this moment to appear in the doorway and have a deliberate coughing fit all the way through the boy's speech.

'It looks like we're still suffering the slings and arrows of outrageous Amelia,' Evie whispers to me.

'At least she didn't actually step inside the studio today,' I point out. 'She probably doesn't want to get attacked by spiders, parrots, frogs or anything else!'

Fortunately the boy with the electric guitar now performs a solo which drowns out Amelia's coughing and everything else. I notice Miss Peabody cover her ears with her hands.

'Wow!' I enthuse. 'He's really good.'

'He's amazing!' Evie agrees. 'I might as well give up now! Forget "Greensleeves". Liam even said I'm playing a really simplified version of it because the real thing would be too hard for me. I'm hopeless!'

'Oh, Evie! Don't say that! I love "Greensleeves"!'

'Er, you do? You're not just saying that to cheer me up?'

'No! You've got to suspend the inner critic! Be positive! Oh, Evie! Wouldn't it be great if Liam would join in? It would be so cool if The Rock Hyraxes were to play at the talent show.'

Evie shakes her head. 'It's not going to happen,' she says, sadly. 'He's still not talking to me. I really think he should get over the whole boys' loos thing—it's not like it's such a big deal. It's a bit sad that he's not supporting Tree-aid because he's worried that his friends will tease him.'

'But I'm sure they wouldn't,' I exclaim. 'Some of the Sixth-Form girls bought wristbands yesterday—and they're cool.'

'I think it's the other members of The Rock Hyraxes that he's mainly worried about,' Evie says. 'I remember him saying that they want to get away from the whole hippie, New Age thing—so Tree-aid doesn't fit with their image. And of course he likes to act like we're not related when we're at school—you should know that by now. So I guess he's unlikely to support anything that I'm involved with at school.'

I heave a sigh. It seems like a waste of several opportunities: an opportunity for Liam and his band to perform, an opportunity for him to support Tree-aid AND his sister, an opportunity for me to give him a big hug . . .

Miss Peabody bursts in on my musings to tell us excitedly that she has just had a word outside in the corridor with Mrs Balderdash and Mr Pomfrey, head of music and drama, and a date has now been set for the talent show. It will take place in the main hall at seven-thirty p.m. on Friday, November fifteenth.

'Two weeks after half-term!' Evie exclaims. 'That's so soon! At least it means I'll still have a good tan from my holiday, which will look good at the show. And do you think there's room for two guitarists in this show?'

'Certainly. Because you've got completely different styles of playing. Your style is—er—unique . . .' I force a smile which I suspect looks more like a grimace. 'We're going to have to rehearse like mad,' I say to Miss Peabody, sounding slightly panicky.

'I'll be here every lunchtime between now and then,' Miss Peabody reassures us. 'So anyone who wants to can come along and rehearse—or audition. And Mr Pomfrey said he'll help—he'll sort out the lighting and sound too. Nearer the time we'll rehearse in the main hall, and we might fit in a few after-school rehearsals as well, for those of you who are very busy at lunchtimes.'

'Do we get out of any lessons, Miss?' Lee wants to know.

Miss Peabody laughs. 'Maybe, nearer the time,' she says.

*   *   *

'So it's really happening!' says Evie.

'Yes—it suddenly seems a lot more real, now that we've got an actual date,' I agree.

We are in the Resource Centre, printing out posters to publicise the talent show.

'I'm quite pleased with this—what do you think?' I say, holding up the poster:

LET ME GREEN-TERTAIN YOU!
THE GREEN-TERTAINERS
ARE PROUD TO PRESENT
A TALENT SHOW
IN THE MAIN HALL

ON FRIDAY, NOVEMBER 15TH AT 7.30 p.m.
IN SUPPORT OF TREE-AID
PARENTS WELCOME!

'I like the green background, and the trees up either side,' says Evie. 'It's cool. Let's go and stick them up everywhere.'

Eco-info

In twenty-four hours worldwide deforestation releases as much CO_2 into the atmosphere as eight million people flying from London to New York. Stopping the logging is the fastest and cheapest solution to climate change.

CHAPTER NINE

It is only four days to go until we both go on holiday. I am excited that it is nearly my birthday, but sorry that I shall be spending it in a field in Cornwall and not with Evie in the sun.

'Only four days to go until I'm lying by a pool, surrounded by palm trees, sipping a long cool drink with a little cocktail umbrella in it,' says Evie.

'Only four days to go until I'm in the middle of a field, surrounded by cows, in the pouring rain, holding an umbrella,' I reply.

*   *   *

With only three days to go Evie says that she's been feeling really guilty about all the carbon emissions because of her family's holiday, so she's been trying to make up for it by turning off as many lights and household appliances as possible.

'Liam went mad because I turned off

his laptop when he was halfway through a game of *Doom Raider*,' she tells me. 'Mum went mad because I turned off the oven and her sponge cake sank. Dad went mad because I switched off the breadmaker and his sun-dried tomato and herb bread turned into a sun-dried tomato and herb splat. They all went mad because I switched the TV off at the mains when it was halfway through recording the concluding episode of the crime drama they've all been watching. So I went mad and told them off for being so dependent on electricity which is making our carbon footprint bigger and bigger.'

'Don't worry!' I say. 'I shall be doing enough carbon-offsetting for both of us on my family's eco-holiday. Dad is seriously worrying me—he wants us to eat only food we gather ourselves from the woods while we are on holiday. What does he MEAN? If he's expecting me to eat a squirrel . . . So I've told him I'm definitely going vegetarian.'

*　　*　　*

With only two days to go Evie asks me why I wasn't at the rehearsal today.

'Miss Grizlingham gave me a lunchtime detention for desk-ercising during graphics again,' I reply.

'Don't do it again!' Evie exclaims. 'We need our rehearsal time. Girls United actually sang in tune today and everyone was amazed! But Amelia annoyed us again—she kept doing a slow handclap. It really put Shaheen off, and she said she can't do her dance if Amelia's going to ruin everything.' Evie sighs. 'What is Amelia's problem? Jack seems to fancy her, which makes everything worse. Because if we boot Amelia out, Jack might go too, and we don't want to lose him because he's good. Why can't Miss Peabody stop her?'

'It's a worry,' I agree. 'I'm waking up thinking about the talent show—and Amelia—and I'm going to bed thinking about the talent show—and Amelia.'

'Perhaps we both need a holiday . . .' says Evie.

103

*   *   *

With only one day to go, I'm thinking about my birthday and how much I am going to miss Evie.

'Only five days to go until I'm a teenager!' I exclaim.

'I know, I know! You're going to be a teenager first,' says Evie, playfully pushing me. 'You've only told me so a hundred times. But I'll be a teenager, too, in January.'

'I love birthdays—but I wish you were going to be with me on the day, Evie. It won't be the same without you.' I chew my lower lip apprehensively. 'It's less than twenty-four hours to go until my family goes eco-mad in the countryside. A zero-carbon holiday. Well, apart from driving there, I suppose.'

'I'll be thinking of you on your birthday,' says Evie.

'While you lie by the pool,' I can't help saying.

'Do you want your present now or when you get back?' Evie asks.

'NOW!' I exclaim.

'Here you are,' says Evie, handing me a tiny, colourful bag. 'Sorry it's not wrapped.'

'Oh—wow!' I squeal. 'It's so tiny! And there's something inside . . .'

'Guatemalan worry dolls,' says Evie. 'I know, it's a really stupid present. But I thought they'd be useful. I know you're too old to play with dolls—you're a TEENAGER—'

'Nearly . . .'

'But these dolls are to tell your worries to. And I'll bring you back something better from my holiday, I promise.'

'Thanks, Evie! The dolls are really cute. I'll need something to tell my worries to while you're away. I'm really going to miss you.

'We'll keep in touch,' says Evie firmly. 'Remind your dad to take his laptop—don't forget! Oh, I'm so excited! I can't help it—despite the carbon emissions.'

*   *   *

HOLIDAYTIME!!

Feeling car sick from a long journey in Dad's van, I settle into my little room in the log cabin at the Mystic Stones eco-retreat. It is comfortable and there is a nice smell of wood. I draw back the red and white checked curtains and look out through the little square window. There isn't a cow in sight. But there is plenty of grass and trees, and a few people walking around and children playing ball outside their holiday cabins. When I open the window I can hear a strange *whoosh! whoosh!* noise which I realise is coming from the wind farm nearby. I close the window again as it is cold outside, and overcast.

'Dad—can I use your laptop?'

'OK, love. Mum and I are just going for a walk to find out where we get the blocks of bio-waste which we're supposed to use for the eco-stove. It's lovely here, isn't it?'

'Yes, Dad.'

Evie has already sent me an email, and over the following days we exchange many more . . .

From: ecoworrierevie
To: ecoworrierlola
Subject: Here I am!

Hi Lola!
Here I am at the Hotel
Splendido on the Costa
Fortuna! Blue skies, blue
sea, palm trees everywhere.
I have to share a room with
Liam (!) but he's being nice
to me now we're on holiday.
He's letting me use his
laptop. I miss you loads.
Wish you were here! Send
reply soon.
    Lots of love,
    Evie xxxxxxxxxxxxxxxx

From: ecoworrierlola
To: ecoworrierevie
Subject: My parents are
completely mad

Hi Evie!
The Hotel Splendido sounds

soooooooo nice! It is raining here. The Mystic Stones eco-retreat is full of people who like to dance around in the rain. Sometimes they sit cross-legged in circles, chanting. Mum has been joining in, which is really embarrassing—I am so glad that none of our friends are here to see this—although I wish you were here with me, Evie. Dad went into the woods to find our supper and came back with some squished blackberries and a dead crow. Mum had a fit so we drove to the nearest town and had fish and chips in the car in the rain. I decided I'm a vegetarian who eats fish. Dad's still trying to get the eco-stove to work so it's cold in our cabin. The loo doesn't flush properly. Miss you loads.

Love you loads,

Lola xxxxxxxxxx
PS: In two days' time I will
be a teenager!

From: ecoworrierevie
To: ecoworrierlola
Subject: Freckles

Hi Lola!
I've been in the sun quite a
lot and I have sooo many
freckles! But I'm being
sensible and using high
factor sun-cream. Mum and
Dad had too much sun
yesterday and have gone red
and crinkly so they're
mainly staying in the shade
today. I bought a Grow Your
Own Palm Tree kit in a shop
so I'll plant it when I get
home to help carbon-offset
this holiday. Feeling guilty
about the emissions. Not
much to do here except laze
by the pool with a long,
cool drink or an ice-cream.

Hope your dad's got the stove working. It sounds like an interesting place where you are—very green and mystical. Missing you.

Love,
Evie xxxxxxxxxxxxxxxx

From: ecoworrierlola
To: ecoworrierevie
Subject: I am a TEENAGER!!!

Hi!!!
It's ME! And I am THIRTEEN today!!! Mum and Dad gave me a beautiful silver chain with a blue pendant on it—and some money to go shopping with! You can come and spend it with me when we get back. I want to go to your mum's shop. Mum and Dad took me for lunch to an Italian restaurant in a seaside town. I decided that I am not a vegetarian when I am in an Italian restaurant.

We had a shock when we got back to our cabin—the eco-stove had blown up and there was bio-waste everywhere. It smelled very strange. We've been given another cabin, although it's smaller and not so nice, and they are coming to clean up our cabin and repair the stove tomorrow. It's cold and cloudy but not raining at the moment. We wear our coats all the time. Miss you!
   Love and kisses,
   Lola xxxxxxxxxxxx

From: ecoworrierevie
To: ecoworrierlola
Subject: Happy birthday!

Hi Lola!
HAPPY BIRTHDAY!!! I can't wait to see you again! There isn't a cloud in the sky—it is soooo lovely here! Sorry

to hear that your stove
exploded but glad you're OK
and that you had a nice
birthday. What's it like,
being a teenager?
  Love and hugs,
  Evie xxxxxxxxxxx

From: ecoworrierlola
To: ecoworrierevie
Subject: I am going mad

Hi Evie!
It isn't as cool, being a
teenager, as you might
think. Today we visited a
goat farm where they make
organic goat's cheese. It
was smelly. Mum felt sick
and Dad has a bad back—he
doesn't like the beds in the
cabin as they're narrow and
hard. Then we visited a
landfill site as part of a
suggested eco-trail. It was
smelly. I think there must
be better ways of getting

the eco-message across—it is putting Mum and Dad right off! Tomorrow is Halloween and I am feeling nervous about spending it in a place called the Mystic Stones— what if this place is really haunted? Mum got a bit upset when she went outside to hang up some washing and a small child took one look at her and ran crying to her mother saying she'd seen a witch. Mum says she thinks that dyeing her hair black was a mistake and she's going to let it go back to its natural colour. Hooray!

We are back in our cabin and the stove is working. Dad is making us goat's cheese on toast. He keeps groaning because of his back. It is pouring with rain outside and now the roof has started to leak. We have put a bucket under the leak and there is a steady drip drip drip. I am really missing you and I am definitely going MAD. I have been talking to the Guatemalan worry dolls quite a lot.

Lola xxxxxxxxxxx

From: ecoworrierevie
To: ecoworrierlola
Subject: Halloween!!!

Hi Lola!
Please let me know that you are OK. The bit about ghosts in your last email really worried me. And I don't want you to go mad. I feel sorry for your mum. She doesn't look anything like a witch. I don't think they have Halloween on the Costa Fortuna. Part of me wants to stay here for ever but mostly I can't wait to see you and get back to preparing for the talent

show!
  Seen you soon and email me sooner!
  Lots of love,
  Evie xxxxxxxxxxxx

From: ecoworrierlola
To: ecoworrierevie
Subject: I'm FINE!

Hi Evie!
Sorry I worried you, but I'm fine. We aren't at the Mystic Stones eco-retreat any longer. Mum had a fit when the loo overflowed and flooded the cabin, so Dad's booked us into this really luxurious seaside hotel for the last two days of our holiday—it even has an indoor pool! Mum and Dad seem a lot more cheerful suddenly.
  See you VERY soon.
  Kisses,
  Lola xxxxxxxxxxxxxxx

Eco-info

Being vegetarian is environmentally friendly. Farmed animals produce more greenhouse gas emissions (largely through their farts!) than the world's transport systems.

CHAPTER TEN

'Thanks, Evie, it's beautiful.' Evie has given me a gorgeous blue bracelet from the Costa Fortuna. 'I can't get over how brown you are!' I exclaim. 'I'm really jealous.'

'Were you jealous all the time I was away?' Evie asks.

'No, not really. I just missed you.'

'I missed you too. How are your mum and dad?'

'Recovering, I think. But they're having some sort of reaction to their green and unpleasant eco-experience, and they've been using loads of heating and hot water since we got back, and then Mum went shopping and came home with all this non-organic food with so much packaging you need a body-builder to wrestle it open. I tried to explain to Mum that our carbon-footprint is going to be huge. I told her that there's more than just food miles to worry about—there's production, processing and packaging as well—but she wouldn't listen.'

'So the zero-carbon holiday backfired.'

'Yes, I think it put them off. But it's made me more determined to get the eco-message across in a fun way, in a way that makes people really want to be green.'

'Hopefully the talent show will do that,' says Evie. 'People will enjoy the show and then they'll be in the right mood to give loads of money to Tree-aid to stop deforestation.'

'That's the plan, as long as Amelia doesn't wreck it!'

'Oh, how can she possibly do that? She's pathetic. Let's not waste any more time even thinking about her,' says Evie, tossing her curls.

'We're going to have to persuade Shaheen to ignore her,' I comment.

'We'll make sure she leaves Shaheen alone,' says Evie confidently.

We are walking to school in a light drizzle. There is a cold wind blowing.

'It's certainly more difficult to persuade people about the danger of global warming when the weather's like this,' I remark.

'That's true,' says Evie. 'It feels really cold, especially after all that warm sun on holiday. I need some warmer clothes!'

'So do I!' I agree, shivering.

'I told Mum that you're planning to spend your birthday money in her shop,' says Evie. 'She was really pleased.'

We pass Amelia who is standing by the main noticeboard staring at one of our talent show posters.

'I hope you're not thinking of doing anything to that poster!' growls Evie. Amelia has defaced posters in the past, and she tore down the ones which we put up in town over the summer to advertise a Fun Day at the Eco Gardens.

Amelia looks at us and twitches her lips in a superior sort of smile, but she doesn't say anything.

'That was weird,' I whisper to Evie when Amelia has gone. 'Normally she'd have a go at us. Do you think she's up to something?'

'Perhaps she's a reformed character,'

says Evie, breezily.

'Are you being serious?'

'No.'

*   *   *

It is good to get back to rehearsals in the drama studio.

'Welcome back, everyone!' trills Miss Peabody. 'I hope you all had a lovely half-term. We now have two weeks to get our acts together! Lola and Evie are in charge, and you must listen carefully because they will be introducing your acts and giving you directions. I also thought that Jack could come on at intervals during the show to perform some of his lovely eco-raps. What do you think?'

Somehow the words 'lovely' and 'rap' do not go together, but we let it pass. Everyone, including Jack, thinks that it is a good idea. Megan and Tegan cheer loudly.

Skye, Megan, Tegan, Karlie, Chelsey, Yasmin and Aisha are all very excited. They tell Miss Peabody that they have been practising their dance during half-term and they think that it is much better now. They are already wearing their Firedance costumes, so Miss Peabody tells them to go ahead. The dance goes well until the end. This time, when the girls bend over, the letters on their backsides spell *ER A DIET*. Everyone collapses in fits of mirth.

Everyone else has been practising as well, with varying degrees of success, but I definitely feel that the whole show is beginning to take shape. Evie feels encouraged, too.

The sun has come out from behind the clouds, and we eat our packed lunches under the school tree, even though it is cold outside. 'Poor school tree!' I say, patting its trunk affectionately. 'I hope you're not too lonely, all on your own. I'm sure you'd like some friends.'

Evie is eyeing me suspiciously. 'So you've started talking to trees,' she says. 'Did something happen to you at the Mystic Stones place—a blow to the head with a mystic stone, perhaps? I know you said you were going mad . . .'

'I happen to have a connection with nature,' I retort. 'Trees have spirits, you know. They deserve our respect and our consideration. You should talk to your oak trees. And the acorn. Don't forget the acorn.'

'Lola,' says Evie. 'You're scaring me.'

I start giggling. I am in a happy mood because preparations for the talent show are going so well. Climbing up on the bench around the school tree, I throw my arms around it and give it the big fat hug that it deserves for putting up with being stuck in the middle of Shrubberylands Comprehensive.

At that precise moment Liam walks past with his friends. He gives me a look which makes me shrivel up, wither and die inside, even though on the outside I have a strange fixed grin on my face. My face is warming up like a ring on an electric cooker.

Liam hurries away, followed by his friends who are all laughing. I hear one of them say the words 'tree-hugger'.

'Oh, great,' says Evie. 'Just when Liam was beginning to get over the whole boys' toilets incident.'

I want to rush after Liam and tell him that I was just fooling around, and that I would much rather hug HIM than hug a tree, if I were to be given the choice, but I know that this would only make matters worse. If they can possibly be worse . . .

*   *   *

Evie comes to my house after school. I don't want to risk bumping into Liam, as I am still embarrassed about hugging the school tree.

I give Evie the smooth, polished blue/grey stone necklace on a thin string, which I have brought back from Cornwall for her.

'Thanks, Lola! It's really beautiful. Is it a mystic stone?'

'It might be, I'm not sure.'

I lie on my bed doodling on a pad of fluorescent green leaf-shaped Post-it notes while Evie puts on the necklace and looks at herself in the mirror. I'm glad she likes the necklace but she spends so long admiring her reflection

123

that I begin to get bored. In exasperation I tear off a few leaf-shaped Post-it notes and stick them in Evie's hair.

'Stop it!' she exclaims. 'You've made me look like a tree!'

We both start giggling. 'I'm a tree!' shouts Evie. 'Give me a hug!'

I give her a hug, and then collapse laughing on to my bed.

'Hang on a minute!' says Evie, looking at herself in the mirror again. 'I've just had an idea! We could dress up as trees to help publicise the talent show and raise awareness for Tree-aid. It would be a good way to attract attention and sell tickets.'

'Dress up as trees?' I repeat, staring at her incredulously. 'And you said that I was mad? Your brother already thinks I'm an idiot. I am NOT dressing up as a tree!'

Evie looks doubtful. 'Perhaps you're right,' she says. 'But we needn't look too mad. Mum's got some long-sleeved brown tops which we could wear with brownish tights and dark shorts or something, so our bodies would be the tree-trunks. And we could use green face paint and stick those leaf Post-it notes in our hair . . . Oh, come on! It would be fun! You were raving about trees earlier today—wouldn't you like to be one?'

'Frankly, no. Amelia and the So Cool Girls would have a field day, poking fun at us.'

'You shouldn't let yourself be intimidated by Amelia and her stupid friends,' says Evie, whose green eyes have the determined glint in them which I know so well.

But I would much rather look cool than look like a tree. After all, I am a teenager now.

Eco-info

Thirteen billion plastic bags are given away in Britain every year, of which 8 billion end up in landfill. Try to take your own bag with you when you go shopping, and reuse plastic bags as much as possible.

CHAPTER ELEVEN

'I have a very bad feeling about this,' I mutter to Evie as I jog to school, earlier than usual. My bag is bulging with the tree costume which Evie has eventually worn me down into bringing, with her coaxing and nagging. My last remaining hope is that Miss Peabody will be sane and sensible and say 'no' when we ask her permission to dress up as trees.

'It'll be fun!' gasps Evie who is struggling to keep up with me. 'Can't you slow down a bit? I mean, it's great that we walk to school, which is more eco-friendly than going by car or bus or train, but do we have to run?'

'You're right,' I say, slowing right down to a reluctant c-r-e-e-p. 'Why should I be in a hurry to dress up as a tree and be the laughing stock of the whole school?'

'Stop saying things like that!' Evie exclaims. 'You're making me nervous. I think we're going to look cool in

Mum's brown tops and our black shorts over brown tights—what's wrong with that?'

'Nothing. I suppose. But it's the green face paint, Post-it notes in the hair and "Hello, I'm a tree" bit that's worrying me.'

*   *   *

'What a brilliant idea, girls!' shrills Miss Peabody. 'Of course you can dress up as trees to raise awareness of the Tree-aid show! I'm sure it will attract a lot of attention! How clever of you! And you've even brought your costumes—well done! Would you like to go and get changed? I can't wait to see you dressed up! I'll go to the staffroom and explain to the other teachers why you'll be dressed as trees today!'

My heart sinks. Miss Peabody is NOT sane and sensible.

*   *   *

In the girls' changing rooms Evie is

getting cold feet. People are already pointing at us, giggling and whispering together.

'I don't think this green face paint goes with my hair,' Evie says in a worried voice, peering in the mirror. 'What kind of tree has orangey-red curly hair?'

'It's autumn,' I say. 'Your leaves are turning to red and gold.'

'That's really poetic!' Evie says, looking happier.

'Yes,' I agree. 'Stupid, but poetic. Stop sticking Post-it notes in my hair! I've got enough!'

'You're a very leafy tree.'

I protest, and Evie agrees that we don't need Post-it notes in our hair. I agree to let her wash off the green face paint. Now we look almost normal!

Evie hesitates. 'What do we do now?'

'Why are you asking me? It was your idea! I suppose we walk around making tree noises.'

'Tree noises? Don't be silly, Lola! All we need to do is say to people "Support Tree-aid! Buy a ticket to the best talent show ever on November fifteenth!" Stuff like that.'

The first bell goes.

'Are we supposed to go to lessons looking like this? I'm not convinced that brown tops and black shorts are a good look—especially when everyone else is in school uniform. Do we have to do this?'

'Yes, we do!' says Evie, taking a deep breath and regaining her enthusiasm. 'Remember that we're dressed like this to support Tree-aid and stop deforestation in Africa and South America—and to sell tickets. We're getting a serious message across in a fun way. That's got to be a good thing!'

* * *

Everyone turns to stare as we walk into the classroom. I feel my cheeks burning up, bright red and hot as fire. I am a tree that blushes!

'Er, support Tree-aid!' Evie says, her voice high-pitched and squeaky. 'Help to save the rainforests and all the creatures who live in the trees in the,

129

er, rainforest! That's why we're dressed as trees,' she adds, by way of explanation.

'Make deforestation history,' I croak, my heart beating very fast. Why do I sound like a frog? When my heart returns to its normal position from my throat, where it has leapt in fright, I gulp and try again: 'Show your support and come to the talent show on November fifteenth.' This time I sound normal—what a relief! 'Stopping global warming can be fun,' I announce, hopefully.

'Let us Green-tertain you!' Evie and I chorus together—we planned this when we were walking to the classroom/to our doom.

The class erupts into laughter and excited chatter. Does this mean that we have successfully got our message across in a fun way? With a slight lurch in my stomach I notice Amelia at the back of the class. She is staring at us and grinning in an unfriendly way. She gives us a sarcastic thumbs up, and then slowly turns her thumb downwards. The So Cool Girls copy her. They are all laughing like hyenas, clutching their middles and nearly falling off their chairs with over-loud laughter.

A rather startled-looking supply teacher called Mr Baines struggles to restore order, and tells us to go and sit down.

There is suppressed giggling throughout the lesson, which is maths. When Mr Baines asks the class a question, Evie calls out the answer and he reminds her to put her hand up next time.

'Don't you mean she should put her branch up, sir?' asks Lee, who is the class clown. This is an excuse for further widespread mirth at our expense.

'I think a bird's made a nest in your hair, Evie!' Amelia calls out. 'Oh, sorry! That's just your natural frizz!'

'Be quiet!' shouts Mr Baines.

I was soooo right to have a bad feeling about today.

*   *   *

'Oh NO!' I moan, clutching Evie's arm—or her branch.

'What is it, Lola?'

We are walking down the main corridor at morning break, trying to interest people in Tree-aid and the talent show—although people don't seem to want to know, which is strange. Are our tree costumes putting people off? The only person who doesn't seem to be put off is the eco-Dalek who, annoyingly, has started following us around, carbon-neutralising people. It is probably the eco-Dalek who is putting people off.

'Liam!' I squeak. 'I can see Liam—and he's coming this way. He already thinks I'm mad, Evie, I don't want him to see me dressed as a tree. Help!'

Evie rolls her eyes. 'Oh, for goodness' sake!' she exclaims, opening a nearby cupboard door and pushing me inside with a load of brooms and buckets—it is quite a squeeze. 'I'll deal with my brother—although I don't know why he worries you so much.' She closes the cupboard door. It is very dark in the cupboard, and there is a strong smell of dust and old socks.

A few seconds later she opens the cupboard door again. 'You don't fancy him, do you?' she asks.

It is my turn to roll my eyes at Evie. 'As IF!' I say. I hope I say it convincingly. I really don't want Evie to know that I spend far too many of my waking hours dreaming of hugging her brother.

'Good,' says Evie, closing the cupboard door again. 'Can I go in the cupboard, too?' I hear the eco-Dalek ask.

'No,' says Evie.

I hold my breath as I hear Liam and his friends walk past the broom cupboard talking. I hear him stop and ask Evie why she has to be so weird. I hear her explaining about dressing up as a tree to raise awareness . . . It is hard to hear what she and Liam are saying . . . They are having a hushed conversation . . . I hear Amelia's name being mentioned . . . I press my ear against the door, straining to hear . . . I press too hard on the door which has not latched properly . . . It opens . . . I fall forward . . . A broom and bucket fall with a clatter . . .

I emerge from the cupboard struggling to keep my balance, and try to look casual, as if hiding in broom cupboards is perfectly normal behaviour.

Liam asks me if I am OK. Oh no! I don't want him to be nice, because if he is nice to me now I will start giggling like an idiot and possibly hug him.

'Oh, I'm fine!' I say airily, aware that I am turning bright red.

Liam and his friends wander off, leaving Evie and the eco-Dalek staring at me with expressions of dumbstruck horror on their faces.

'Er, don't feel you have to cheer me up or anything like that,' I say. 'Just carry on staring at me as if I'm something that just crawled out of a landfill site—I really don't mind.'

Evie and the eco-Dalek don't move. They don't say anything.

'Now you're scaring me. So why aren't you doubled up with laughter at my expense?'

'Oh, Lola!' Evie blurts out at last.

'It's awful!'

'I know it is—I just fell out of a broom cupboard. But I guess I'll get over it in time. Thanks for being so concerned, but you're actually making me feel worse—'

'No—you don't understand!' says Evie desperately. 'Liam just told me that Amelia's been telling everyone that her dad's going to have a fashion show to launch his range of clothes, and it's happening on the same night as the talent show. It clashes completely! She's been putting up notices. Her dad's show is taking place at the Shrubberylands Travel Inn! It's a disaster!'

'Oh,' I say, doubtfully. 'But surely no one's going to want to go to a rubbish fashion show—'

'But they are!' moans Evie. 'Amelia's also been telling people that Jadene the supermodel is going to be there, modelling some of her dad's clothes— and her dad wants a few extra models to take part and has invited anyone from the school who fancies their chances of being a model to go along to the Travel Inn on Saturday to audition. Amelia's been bragging that she'll be doing some of the modelling, and that Jadene has given her private coaching on how to be a model. Liam says that everyone's talking about it— he seemed really excited at the prospect of seeing Jadene! Oh, Lola, no one's interested in Tree-aid or the talent show any more!'

'I am,' says the eco-Dalek.

'OK . . .' I say, thinking hard. 'Surely it's not such a big problem? We just go to Miss Peabody and ask her to change the date of the talent show. Come on!'

But when we find Miss Peabody and ask her if the date can be changed, she shakes her head and says that the hall has been booked and we've sold some tickets, even if we haven't sold that many, so it's too late to change the date.

'But I'm sure lots of people will still come to the show, especially now that they've seen you in your wonderful tree costumes!' says Miss Peabody, encouragingly.

I wish I shared her optimism.

136

*   *   *

On the way back to lessons we see that Amelia has stuck the poster advertising her dad's fashion show over the top of our Green-tertainers poster. The poster also advertises for people to come to the Travel Inn on Saturday and audition to be a model at the show.

People are already strutting up and down the corridors and round the playground, striking poses, pouting and practising for the modelling auditions.

'It's so unfair! We've really only had success with the lower school, but everybody seems to be interested in Amelia's dad's show!' Evie exclaims indignantly, her cheeks flushing angrily. 'Why does Amelia always have to wreck everything?'

'She couldn't stand the fact that we were getting more attention than she was,' I comment. 'So she had to muscle in and steal the limelight. Look out,' I say, nudging Evie with my elbow. 'Here she comes. I think we should act like we're not bothered. Don't give her the satisfaction of knowing that she's seriously winding us up. Like I said before, she just wants a reaction.'

'You're right,' says Evie, and we start to walk away.

But Amelia comes slithering after us like a big snake, spitting venom.

'Running away, are you?' she calls out. 'Don't you realise how stupid you look in your pathetic tree costumes?'

Evie stops and turns to face Amelia, giving her a bored and contemptuous look. 'What's your problem, Amelia?'

Amelia puts her hands on her hips. 'I'm not the one with a problem!' she sneers. 'You two losers are sooooo uncool! I told you that my dad would put your mum's sad little shop in the shade.' Evie's face darkens. 'My dad's clothes are so cool,' Amelia continues. 'You should come along to the launch next week and see the whole collection. Oh—I forgot! You can't, because you'll be prancing around on a stage that night, dressed as trees. It's probably just as well. I don't think you'd make it as models for my dad's show—you haven't got "the look". Jadene says that

138

you need to have "the look" to be a model. She says that I've got "the look".'

If Amelia's skin wasn't as thick as rhino hide, "the look" which Evie is currently giving her would have killed her stone dead several seconds ago.

'You're pathetic, Amelia!' Evie says, her face thunderous and her green eyes flashing.

Amelia twitches her lips in a sort of smirk, but doesn't say anything. She is looking at someone standing just behind us. Turning, I see Jack standing a short distance away.

'Hi, Jack!' says Amelia in a flirty, little girly voice. Seeing us, Jack looks sheepish. Amelia lightly skips towards him, they link arms and wander away without another word, although Amelia flings us a final evil look over her shoulder.

'What the . . . ?' exclaims Evie.

'Amelia has all the subtlety of a gorilla wielding a sledgehammer,' I comment.

'But how could Jack possibly bear to be with her?' Evie asks, incredulously.

'He's supposed to be the Master of Ceremonies for our show—I feel like he's a kind of traitor, flirting with the enemy.'

I shrug and pull a 'don't-ask-me' face. 'Jack's a louse,' I say. 'Just give him a piece of tree bark to live under. He's probably hoping to meet Jadene, like all the other boys.' I feel a pang in my stomach when I remember that Liam is one of Jadene's biggest fans. Does Liam only like supermodels? I am never likely to be a supermodel.

*   *   *

Not many people turn up to the rehearsal at lunch-break.

'I wonder where everyone is?' Miss Peabody wonders. 'Is there something going on?'

I feel too dispirited to talk about what's going on. Evie is silent, too, which is not like Evie.

Our spirits rise when Skye, Megan, Tegan, Karlie, Chelsey, Yasmin and Aisha spill into the room, but they sink again when Skye tells Miss Peabody that she and the other members of Firedance are dropping out of the show because they want to go to Amelia's dad's fashion show and see Jadene.

'And we're hoping that some of us will get to do some modelling!' says Tegan, excitedly.

'So you're deserting the show,' says Evie, sounding hurt and angry.

Tegan and the other girls look awkward. 'Er, perhaps we can do a show another time!' says Skye, and they leave hurriedly.

'There's going to be no one left to be in the show!' Evie howls. 'There's not going to be a show. Everyone's deserting us!'

'I'm not,' says the eco-Dalek.

'I'm still here,' says Harry. 'And Eddie's not here because he's gone to the dentist. But he'll still want to bring Rico and Norman and be in the talent show. He's not into supermodels—he prefers frogs and parrots.'

'Fine,' says Evie. 'So we've got a magician, a frog, a parrot, an eco-Dalek, a few bad jokes and some music which no one cares about or is the tiniest bit interested in. And we've only sold about ten tickets so we won't be raising any money or awareness for Tree-aid, and Mr Woodsage won't have a nice surprise.'

I put my arm round Evie's shoulders—I am afraid that she is going to cry. 'You've forgotten about Cassia, Ellen and Salma,' I say consolingly. 'I'm sure they won't desert us.'

At this moment Ellen comes into the room and reassures us that they would never let us down. Evie smiles wanly.

Miss Peabody looks worried. 'Don't despair, Evie,' she says. 'Not everyone will be going to Amelia's father's fashion show. I'm sure people will start coming back to us soon, after the excitement's died down. Let's give it a day or two, shall we?'

*   *   *

Evie and I go to the girls' changing room and change out of our tree costumes. I never thought I would feel glad to wear my uniform!

'I've had enough of being a tree,' I say. 'I told you it was a bad idea.'

Evie turns on me angrily. 'It was only a bad idea because of Amelia,' she retorts. 'I can do without you having a go at me.'

'I'm not having a go at you. I'm just upset—that's all.'

Evie stuffs her tree costume into her bag and leaves the changing room without me.

'Evie! Don't be like that!' But when I go out into the corridor, she has already gone.

There are still a few minutes left until afternoon lessons, so, feeling doubly upset now that I have fallen out with Evie, I take refuge in the Resource Centre where it is always quiet and peaceful. Shaheen is just leaving. She tells me that she still wants to do her dance and she couldn't be happier that Amelia will be out of the way at her dad's show on the night of the talent show, but she is worried when I tell her that a lot of our acts seem to be drifting away. Then she leaves, after putting some unwanted sheets of paper in the recycling bin. I am glad that some people are getting the message about going green.

I sit down at a computer and find Amelia's dad's website. I remember the address from the summer when Evie and I looked at his website when he was causing trouble for the Eco Gardens.

The David Plunkett website charts Amelia's dad's meteoric rise in the world of business. There is a page on his website headed *Plunkett's Fashion Bargainstore*. I feel puzzled. Would a top supermodel really be attracted by a collection called Plunkett's Fashion Bargainstore? But David Plunkett is a very rich man—he probably offered her lots of money. I click on to the Fashion Bargainstore page which leads on to other pages full of photos of trendy skirts, trousers, tops, dresses, belts and bags. They are the sort of clothes which would probably appeal to footballers' wives and other celebrities. A whole page is devoted to just one item—a long-sleeved white jumper with a scoop neck and flecks of gold thread running through it and a row of three little gold buttons down the front. It is described as *This season's must-have fashion bargain!*

I sigh heavily. The website hasn't really told me anything useful—I'm not even sure why I looked at it. I want to make things up with Evie, and the bell has just gone, so I grab my bag and head back to lessons . . .

Eco-info

About 3 million tonnes of plastic are thrown out every year in the UK—and only 7% is currently recycled. The rest goes to landfill sites where the plastic can take up to 500 years to decompose.

CHAPTER TWELVE

It has been a bad week. Evie has been despondent and has not been keen to talk to me even though I said that I was sorry and offered to lend her my Seven Shades of Blue organic eye-shadow kit which I know that she has wanted to borrow for ages.

The whole school is in the grip of Jadene fever, which has completely overshadowed the talent show. Another act—Girls United—has dropped out. We now have only seven acts—and one of them is Evie! The other six are Lee the comedian, Cassia, Ellen and Salma's gymnastics display, Dan the cool guitarist, Harry and his magic, Eddie and his tree-frog and parrot, and Shaheen dancing—hardly enough for a whole show, although it might still be possible. But it is disappointing.

On Wednesday, I confronted Jack when I saw him coming out of the canteen without Amelia, who keeps following him trying to take him away from us. I am afraid that she has succeeded.

Me: 'I thought you wanted to be in our show?'

Jack: 'Er, it's a bit awkward . . .'

Me: 'So you're going to let us all down, just so you can go and drool over Jadene AND Amelia!'

Jack: 'I don't drool
    It's not cool.'

Me: 'Don't you DARE rap at me!'

I am quite proud of myself for giving Jack, one of the coolest boys in Year Eight, a piece of my mind, but it didn't really help. Like most of the boys, Jack seems fascinated by Jadene and probably thinks that he can get to her through Amelia.

It rained heavily all day on Wednesday, which was Bonfire Night, and the fireworks display at the rugby club had to be cancelled.

To make matters worse, Evie, who has rather grudgingly started talking to me today, tells me that Liam has been raving about Jadene all week, and it is driving her MAD.

We walk home together. I have been jogging home all week and leaving Evie behind, sulking. But I am fed up with the frostiness between us, and am keen to encourage the fact that she has started talking to me again.

'I'm sorry I've been in a mood,' says Evie as we link arms. 'But I've been feeling so stressed about the talent show.'

'Me too,' I say. 'But we should be sticking together—let's not fall out again.'

'Agreed,' says Evie. 'Eco-worriers will triumph together!'

'Maybe . . .'

'There's a saying—"Don't get mad—get even!" Wouldn't it be great if we could get even with Amelia?'

'Yes—but I don't see how . . .'

We walk in silence for a few minutes.

'Mum sorted out some clothes for us to wear at the show the other day. But I wasn't very grateful—I wouldn't even try them on. I feel sorry now. Would you like to come in and see them?'

I say 'yes' even though I am worried about bumping into Liam after the tree-falling-out-of-a-broom-cupboard incident. Fortunately Liam doesn't seem to be around.

Evie's mum's friend, Wanda, is in the kitchen with Evie's mum, drinking coffee. Wanda is a journalist working for the *Shrubberylands Sentinel*, and she helped us to expose Plunkett's lies about the Eco Gardens.

Evie tells Wanda about the talent show, and Wanda offers to cover it. She notices that Evie seems subdued, and we explain about Plunkett's fashion show clashing with the Green-tertainers.

'Oh, what a shame!' Wanda exclaims. 'I remember now—David Plunkett contacted the *Sentinel* a few days ago and asked us to cover his show.'

She explains that one of the *Shrubberylands Sentinel*'s junior reporters is going along to cover it and write an article, but David Plunkett has made it clear that Wanda is NOT welcome as he has obviously not forgiven her.

'I suppose clothes are more eco-friendly than his usual Plunkett's

Plastics rubbish,' Wanda remarks.

'Not necessarily,' says Evie. 'They're probably produced in sweatshops by child labourers.'

Wanda takes a sip of coffee. 'I'm not sure how we'd prove that,' she says. 'I don't suppose there's anything on his website to say where the clothes come from.'

'No, there isn't,' I say.

'That instantly makes me suspicious,' says Wanda. 'I'll see what I can find out.'

'Thanks, Wanda.'

*　　　*　　　*

'The show must go on!' I say to Evie, as we relax in her room, listening to Boys Next Door.

'But how? At least we know that one person is coming—Wanda!'

Evie, who has been staring hard at her latest List of Things to Worry About, suddenly rips it into little pieces and throws them in the air, where they fall like confetti to the floor.

'What's the point of worrying?' she

150

says, lying back on her bed.

'That's an unusual thing for an eco-worrier to say,' I remark.

'I know. But I've been thinking. We just need the right attitude—attitude is a small thing which makes a big difference.'

'I can't help feeling that an audience would be useful, too,' I say, with a sigh.

'We'll get Mum and Wanda and your parents to invite all their friends. And I'll just have to play more stuff on my guitar, and Dan can play more stuff, Harry can do loads of magic—and at least we've got Norman the tree-frog! How can we fail?'

'Are you serious?'

'Half-serious. But I'm serious about one thing.'

'What's that?'

'We're not going to let Amelia have the last laugh . . . Eco-worriers are going to fight back!'

Eco-info

Cutting down trees can cause flooding as trees absorb water from the ground and create a natural barrier to rivers. In some forest areas, the sun-blocking tree canopy keeps the ground from drying out and becoming barren desert.

CHAPTER THIRTEEN

'I don't know what to choose—your mum's clothes are so lovely!' I say to Evie.

We are in Fashion Passion where I have come with Evie to spend my birthday money. Evie is wearing a blue and green stripy jumper today which comes from her mum's shop.

Finally, after extensive browsing—Evie is beginning to yawn—I choose a reduced *Love, Peace and Harmony* T-shirt, a pink top with a red heart on it, a black yak's wool mini-skirt, and a cropped fluffy red jumper which is funky and also a good idea as the weather is cold and overcast although it is not raining. I want to leave enough money for some ethically-manufactured make-up and bath stuff, and some ice-cream for Evie and me. I hope Meltonio will still be selling ice-creams—he works in his brother's café when the weather gets too cold for ice-cream.

Evie's mum gives me an extra twenty per cent discount—and an incredible green silk scarf. 'That's a birthday present,' she says, smiling.

'Oh—thank you so much! It's really beautiful!'

I go into the changing cubicle and put on all my new clothes—they look a bit weird together, but I am so happy, I want to wear all my new things.

As we leave Fashion Passion, we see Amelia walk past. At the same time Jack approaches from the opposite direction. Amelia sidles up to him and tries, very obviously, to make it look as though they are together. Jack looks awkward. I notice that Amelia is wearing 'this season's must-have' white jumper from the Plunkett's Fashion Bargainstore collection under a cropped brown jacket with fake fur collar and cuffs—at least I hope the fur is fake.

I am hoping that she hasn't seen us, but suddenly she turns and looks straight at me.

'Ohmigod—Lola!' she exclaims. 'What happened? You're a fashion disaster! I've always known that you and Evie are uncool, but you've just taken "uncool" to a whole new level!'

'She looks great,' says Evie loyally, leaping to my defence.

'Well, forgive me if I don't worship you as a style icon,' says Amelia sarcastically.

Jack is hanging around a short distance away, looking uneasy.

'Your dad's clothes aren't anything special,' Evie mutters.

'You're only saying that because you wouldn't recognise what's hot and what's not if it got up and hit you between the eyes!' Amelia snaps. 'I happen to be wearing this season's must-have top—anyone who's anyone wants this top—and you can only get it from my dad's collection! Jadene wears this top—she told me it's one of her favourite tops ever!'

'You don't say,' Evie rolls her eyes and folds her arms.

'Loads of people have turned up at the Travel Inn, wanting to audition to be models at my dad's show,' Amelia continues. 'You should go and see.

They're all there at the moment. All those people who were going to be in your sad, pathetic talent show are jostling to get in to see Jadene. You were there just now, weren't you, Jack?'

Jack hangs his head. 'I've got to go,' he mutters.

'Oh, hang on!' says Amelia. 'We'll go together and see Jadene, shall we, Jack?'

Jack avoids meeting my eyes. Evie raises her eyebrows. 'So Jadene's there? Right now?'

'Oh, she's just flown in from the States,' says Amelia. 'She's a bit jet-lagged so she's gone to have a sleep—so she might not make it to the auditions.'

'Right.' Evie stares hard at Amelia, who flicks her long blond hair back and refuses to meet Evie's eyes.

'Jack and I have got to go,' she says. I notice that she is holding on to his arm, and he looks as though he wants to get away. 'It's been lovely talking to you—not. I hope you get a life soon, and some clothes sense. Losers.'

'She always has to have the last word!' I say, as we watch Amelia take Jack by the arm and drag him away through the crowd. Evie does that thing where you make the sign of the cross to ward off vampires.

We can't resist going to the Travel Inn to have a look, even though it is depressing to see so many of the Green-tertainers hanging around in the function room which is being used for the modelling auditions. The whole thing seems disorganised, and many people are sitting around with their parents, on hard plastic chairs, arms folded, looking bored. We spot David Plunkett and Mrs Plunkett at the far end of the room, holding clipboards, and signalling for the next person to walk past them wearing items from the Plunkett's Fashion Bargainstore Collection. The clothes are very fashionable, but they look very similar to items that can be purchased very cheaply from a number of high street chainstores.

*   *   *

'It's awful!' I exclaim suddenly. 'Everyone's there, wanting to be part of Plunkett's fashion show. No one's interested in the talent show any longer. No one's going to turn up. It was a silly idea.'

Evie looks miserable. 'You're probably right. We're uncool Year Eights, and we've probably turned people off the idea of going green.'

Even ice-cream from Meltonio's van, which we find parked near the shopping centre, fails to lift our spirits.

Meltonio says that business is slow. Despite global warming, there is not much demand for ice-cream in November. He tells us that he is going to put the ice-cream van away for the winter, and go to work in his brother's café. But he also tells us that he is going to see Mrs Balderdash next week about supplying the school with ice-cream, and some fruit and vegetables from the allotments. We smile wanly, and thank him.

*   *   *

I am staying at Evie's house tonight. I wanted her to have a sleepover at my house so that I wouldn't have to face Liam, but Mum and Dad are going out to dinner, and they say that it would be better if I stayed with Evie. I am offended that they don't trust us to stay home alone. Mum says that it has nothing to do with trust, and everything to do with responsibility. She says that she wouldn't feel right, leaving us on our own. I am feeling so upset about the talent show that I lose my cool and storm upstairs to get my overnight things, slamming my bedroom door. Evie follows me upstairs, hesitantly opening the door and saying, 'You really ARE a teenager!'

*　　　*　　　*

Evie and I are going to do our homework together. At least it is a distraction from thinking about the talent show. It is an unusual homework. Miss Peabody has asked her geography class to watch a series of programmes about India which are on every Saturday evening. Miss Peabody also records them and we watch highlights during the week, in case anyone has missed it, and have a class discussion.

'Where's Liam?' I ask nervously, as we settle down on the sofa in front of the television. Evie's dad is in the kitchen, preparing something for us to eat, and her mum is at the computer in a corner of the living room.

'Making himself a bacon sandwich, I think,' Evie replies. 'Then he's probably going out. You're not still worried about seeing him, are you?'

'No! Not at all!' I say with a light laugh, glancing over my shoulder towards the living-room door.

The programme about India is about to begin. 'Tonight's documentary on India focuses on the shame of India's sweatshops and the cruelty of child labour. It contains scenes which some viewers may find disturbing,' says the programme announcer.

Evie and I are disturbed and appalled by the shots of dingy and poorly lit back rooms with no windows, crammed with sad-eyed children sewing sequins on to saris and making garments intended for export to shops in the United Kingdom and other countries. The children are under-nourished and their bodies are not developing properly because of being forced to sit cross-legged all day with no chance of exercise.

'These children's childhoods have been sacrificed to produce cheap garments like this,' says the presenter, holding up a white jumper with gold thread running through it and a row of three little gold buttons.

'Did you see that?' Evie exclaims.

'Of course I did!' I say. We are both leaning forward, staring fixedly at the television. Evie's mum has come over to see what it is we're looking at, and Liam has just come into the room with a bacon sandwich—I hardly notice he's there because I am more concerned about what I've just seen.

'Come on!' urges Evie. 'Show it again!'

'Show what?' Liam asks thickly,

through a mouth full of bacon sandwich.

'They just showed one of the garments produced in those horrible sweatshops,' Evie tells him. 'It was one of the tops from Amelia's dad's collection!'

'Are you sure?' Liam asks.

'Yes! Amelia was wearing it. She called it "this season's must-have fashion top"—Oh, look! There it is again!' She points to the screen excitedly.

This time there is a shot of a western model wearing the white jumper.

'That's the same photo that's on the website!' I exclaim.

The documentary switches back to the sweatshop in India, showing the buttons being sewn on to the same garment by a child with sores on his legs from prolonged sitting. Tears spring to my eyes, and both Evie and her mum look very distressed.

'Must be a mistake,' says Liam.

'Let's go on to the Plunkett website and find the top to show Liam so he believes us!' Evie exclaims.

With my assistance, Evie finds the picture of the white jumper. Liam takes a look.

'You're right,' he says. He scratches his head. 'That's really bad,' he mutters, looking awkward. 'Anyway— I've got to go . . .' He leaves.

'He's still hoping to meet Jadene,' says Evie, scornfully. 'He cares more about meeting a stupid supermodel than he does about children used as slave labour in sweatshops!'

'That's a bit harsh, dear,' says Evie's mum. 'I wonder if Wanda's watching this programme. I'll give her a call in a moment and find out. I'm sure she'll be interested.'

Upstairs in Evie's room I can almost hear her brain clicking and whirring and hatching a plan to take revenge on Amelia.

'Everyone in our Year is going to see that programme,' she says. 'We need to draw people's attention to the fact that the jumper shown on the programme is the same as the one in the Plunkett collection. Surely no one's going to want to go near Plunkett's Fashion

Bargainstore collection after that!'

I look doubtful. 'It will put some people off,' I agree. 'But others will still want to buy his clothes, especially since they're cheap and if they think that Jadene wears them. And people are still going to want to meet her.'

Evie sighs. 'I despair!' she says. 'Trees are so much more important than meeting some stupid supermodel. I want to raise money for Tree-aid and help to save the planet from the threat of global warming. And I can't believe we're being stopped from doing that by Amelia's dad's horrible fashion show!'

'Let's listen to Dodo's greatest hits,' I suggest. 'It's good music to despair to . . .'

Eco-info

Too many companies use suppliers who produce goods cheaply because they pay people very little for working very long hours. Some suppliers also have poor factory standards, to save on costs. You can help by checking that the clothes you buy are ethically manufactured.

CHAPTER FOURTEEN

THWUMP!

'Evie! Leave me alone.'

Evie puts down her pillow. 'We didn't have a pillow fight last night,' she says. 'So I thought we'd have one this morning.'

'Don't you think we're getting a bit old for pillow fights?'

Evie regards me thoughtfully. 'You've changed since you became a teenager,' she says.

'No I haven't. I'm just tired.'

'It's nearly midday. I thought you said you wanted to get up early and go for a jog.'

'I changed my mind. Even Olympic hopefuls need a rest occasionally.'

Evie goes to the computer. 'While you were sleeping I read *Green Teen* magazine and then I went on Plunkett's website. He's already removed that picture of this season's must-have white jumper.'

'He must have seen the programme

and been worried that people would recognise it and refuse to buy his stuff.'

'Yes, but it's too late. Loads of people will have seen the programme. Mum's told Wanda about it—I expect Wanda was already watching it. And Miss Peabody's recorded it. So it's not looking good for Amelia!' Evie concludes with satisfaction.

'Do you think that Amelia watched the programme?' I ask.

'I doubt it,' says Evie. 'She only watches programmes like *Pro-Celebrity Underwater Hairdressing.*'

'*Pro-Celebrity Underwater Hairdressing*? That sounds quite interesting. It should have mermaids in it! When's it on?'

Evie rolls her eyes at me. 'I was joking!' she says. 'I just mean that Amelia doesn't watch serious documentaries.'

'Remind me, when do we watch it at school with Miss Peabody?'

'Tuesday, I think.'

'Wouldn't it be great if we had the actual top to show people? With the Plunkett label inside! That would really put Amelia in her place—and it would make more of an impression on people that clothes made in sweatshops are being sold here.'

Evie is sitting cross-legged on the bed, twisting one of her red curls round her finger and chewing her bottom lip. I notice a glint in her green eyes.

'You've had an idea, haven't you?' I say.

'Yes . . .'

*   *   *

Downstairs in the living room Evie's mum and dad are reading the Sunday papers, and Liam is sitting on the sofa wearing a towelling dressing gown, hunched over a steaming cup of coffee. He has obviously just got up. I try not to look at him, but my eyes seem to be irresistibly drawn in his direction. I go cold all over at the thought that I might lose control and hug him, in his dressing gown!

'Lola, you're looking strange again. Are you OK?'

'I'm fine!' I reply, sitting in a chair as

far away from Liam as possible.

'Here—have a magazine to look at. It's one of those trashy celebrity mags—I think it came with the Sunday papers. It's got the TV schedules in the back—have a look and see if they're repeating that programme on India.'

It is a relief to have something to look at to divert my attention away from Liam.

But seconds later I leap to my feet, clutching the magazine, and shouting 'Oh! Evie! You've got to see this! This is so cool!'

Evie looks at me as if I have gone mad. 'Don't tell me you're getting excited by celebrity magazines!' she exclaims. 'I told you—you've changed since you became a teenager. You'd better not turn into one of Amelia's So Cool Girls—I'd never speak to you again.'

'No, it's nothing like that—this is really interesting!' I shove the magazine into her lap and point to a page.

'So what's happened?' says Evie in a bored voice. 'Has someone broken a fingernail? Has someone else had new hair extensions . . . oh . . . OHMIGOD!'

'Now do you see what I mean?'

'Yes,' Evie replies. 'Yes I certainly do.'

We both pore over the magazine. There is a double-page spread with the heading: *YES! IT'S JUNGLE JADENE!* There is a large photo of Jadene wearing a leopard-print bikini and swinging on a vine like Tarzan—or Jane. The accompanying article reads: *The identity of the mystery celeb on next week's* I'm Famous—Rescue Me! *can now be revealed! It is none other than the supermodel Jadene, who jets off to the jungle today! Jadene will be staying in the deep, dark jungle with the other celebrities for the series—I'm sure that her jungle mates will agree that things get hotter in the jungle when Jadene jets in!*

Evie looks at me, open-mouthed. 'So that means—' she begins.

'That Amelia's lying!' I say, finishing the sentence. 'Jadene's in the jungle. She's not here in Shrubberylands. And there's no chance of her modelling

Amelia's dad's poxy clothes on Friday—they don't let them out of the jungle once they're in there. Unless they get evicted. And Jadene's so popular, she'll probably be there for the whole series. She'll probably win!'

Evie shows the article to Liam. He reads it, and then throws the magazine down in disgust, sitting back and folding his arms. 'The lying little so-and-so!' he exclaims. I assume that he means Amelia. 'So Jadene won't be coming to Shrubberylands,' he says.

Evie shakes her head. 'It would seem that she won't.'

'How could Amelia have had the nerve to tell a pack of lies to the whole school?' Liam asks in tones of outrage.

'That's Amelia for you!' Evie replies.

'Or maybe Jadene *was* going to model for Plunkett's collection but immediately something better turned up, like the TV show, she dropped it,' I suggest. 'And Amelia didn't want to admit that she wasn't coming any longer.'

'That's generous of you,' says Evie. 'Giving Amelia the benefit of the

170

doubt.'

'I can't believe I was taken in!' says Liam, shaking his head. 'I feel like such an idiot!'

'We could have told you not to trust her,' says Evie. 'But you never listen to us.'

'OK,' says Liam. 'I'm sorry. Is that what you want me to say?'

Evie smiles a satisfied smile. 'I'd like you to say you'll give me an electric guitar lesson . . .'

*   *   *

Evie is sitting on her bed, practising "Greensleeves" on her guitar after her lesson with Liam. He has given her his old guitar, having recently bought a new one. She seems to have regained her enthusiasm. We are both feeling more optimistic about our chances of going ahead with the talent show as people will have realised that Jadene is in the jungle and will not be at Plunkett's fashion show. They are therefore likely to lose interest in the fashion show—which is good news for the Green-tertainers!

'That was nice of Liam, giving you a guitar,' I say.

'Yes—and I'm hoping he'll be a whole lot nicer very soon,' she says.

'What do you mean?'

'Ah. That would be telling. I don't want to put a jinx on it by telling you. Let's just say I'm going to work on Liam . . .'

'OK.' I am flicking through an old copy of *Green Teen* magazine. I frown. 'Do you think that we should confront Amelia, tell her that we know the truth, and give her the chance to confess to people that she's been lying. That'll make her look really small without making us look too vindictive.'

'The trouble is,' says Evie, 'Amelia's so good at wriggling out of things, and making it seem like she's not a liar.' Evie puts down her guitar and thoughtfully twiddles her curls. 'Ah!' she says suddenly. 'I've just had a BRILLIANT idea!'

'Another one?' I am beginning to feel jealous. Brilliant ideas seem to be pouring out of Evie in all directions.

Isn't it time that I had an idea? But when she tells me about her idea, I have to admit that it is inspired.

Eco-info

The forests in Africa expand very slowly because the land is hot and dry around the edges. New trees mainly grow under the canopy of taller trees, so if the canopy is destroyed it is difficult for new trees to grow.

CHAPTER FIFTEEN

'So did you do your geography homework, Amelia?' Evie calls out, as we pass her in the corridor at school. She is on her own for once.

Amelia turns and gives Evie a withering stare.

'Did you watch that programme on Saturday night about India, like Miss Peabody asked us to?' Evie persists.

'As IF!' Amelia retorts dismissively. 'Some of us have lives, you know. I don't do homework!'

'We know you're lying, Amelia,' Evie says. 'Jadene's in the jungle. She's taking part in *I'm Famous—Rescue Me!*, as I'm sure you already know!'

Amelia hesitates, swallows hard—and then recovers. 'That's right!' she says airily. 'She's jetting back here on Friday in her own private pink jet to take part in my dad's show. Then she'll go back to the jungle.'

'And that's what you're telling people?' I ask.

Amelia shrugs. 'It's the truth,' she says.

'No, it isn't!' I say. 'It's a lie. Sorry, Amelia—we're not as gullible as your so-called So Cool friends. We know you're lying.'

'Yes,' continues Evie. 'And what are you going to tell people when Jadene fails to show up on Friday?'

Amelia hesitates again. 'Er, that there was a problem with her pink jet,' she falters.

Evie folds her arms and gives Amelia a long, hard look. 'I don't know what you're hoping to achieve by spinning out this lie,' she says.

Amelia shrugs. 'What does it matter?' she says. 'My dad's fashion show is still going to be cooler than your stupid talent show. You wouldn't catch me sharing a stage with a frog.'

'Norman's very talented,' says Evie.

'Oh, go and recycle yourselves!' Amelia snaps. She turns her back on us, and marches away.

*   *   *

Miss Peabody is fluttering around the drama studio like a hyperactive butterfly. 'Only four days to go until the show!' she trills excitedly. 'We'll be having a dress rehearsal in the Main Hall on Thursday at lunchtime. And if anyone wants to stay behind and rehearse after school any day this week, I'll be here—and Mr Pomfrey said he'll drop in to help!'

'Er, Miss,' I say. 'There's no one here. There are no acts.'

'Let's just wait a few moments, shall we?' says Miss Peabody nervously. 'I expect people will turn up soon!'

Evie nods. We are all staring towards the doorway to the drama studio, willing people to come through it.

The eco-Dalek arrives, followed by Harry and Eddie. Then Lee arrives. 'I've got some more jokes!' he says.

'Carry on,' says Evie. 'We need cheering up.'

'OK. What do you call a gorilla with a couple of bananas in his ears?'

'I don't know,' says Miss Peabody. 'What do you call a gorilla with a couple of bananas in his ears?'

'Anything you like—he can't hear you!' says Lee.

Miss Peabody shrieks with laughter.

'I've heard that one before,' says Evie.

'That's what makes my jokes eco-friendly,' replies Lee triumphantly. 'They're all recycled!'

'Ha ha.'

'Would you like another one?' Lee looks at us hopefully.

'Go on, then.'

'OK. What's grey and has four legs and a trunk?'

'A mouse going on holiday,' say Harry and Eddie together.

'Oh.' Lee looks disappointed. 'You stole my punch- line!'

We sit in silence for a few minutes. Then Shaheen arrives with her uncle and his sitar! The beautiful dancing and the music have a more cheering effect than Lee's jokes.

While Shaheen is dancing, the guitarist and one of the girl singers come into the studio.

When the dancing is over, the girl singer, whose name is Beth, tells us she didn't enjoy the modelling auditions on Saturday and they didn't think much of Plunkett's fashion collection.

'They looked really cool but they weren't at all well made,' she says. 'The zip broke on the skirt I modelled, and the hem was coming down. There was even a hole in the top I was given to put on.'

Beth and several other people say that they would like to come back and be in the talent show again. Miss Peabody says that she thinks that they've made the right decision.

'It looks like we're going to have a show after all,' I say to Evie, as we walk back to lessons, arm in arm.

'Yes—I just wish some of the other acts would come back. Jack's a pain, but he was good at what he did—I really enjoyed his raps. Surely he doesn't want to go on hanging around with Amelia?'

'He may come back tomorrow,' I say.

'Yes, I hope so,' Evie says.

Eco-info

It has been estimated that, in developing countries, 250 million children between the ages of five and fourteen work, many in sweatshops.

CHAPTER SIXTEEN

On our way to school, I tell Evie that I am having to work hard at coaxing Mum and Dad back into green ways after the shock of our eco-holiday put them off. 'I've got them to agree to install a compost bin in the garden,' I say. 'I think that's a good start. Then I want to get them to get chickens, and a goat. We could be self-sufficient, and grow all our own vegetables.'

Evie laughs. 'Good luck with the chickens and goat,' she says. 'I don't think my parents would agree to that. Especially not the chickens—you know that Mum's not keen on birds. And Liam would probably argue that we're depriving third world chicken farmers of their income.'

I smile. 'Is Liam still helping you with "Greensleeves"?'

'He's helped me a bit. I think it's coming on well.'

*　　　*　　　*

Chairs scrape and the chattering subsides as the class settles down for Miss Peabody's geography lesson.

I notice that Amelia is reading a magazine concealed under her desk. One of the So Cool Girls is painting her nails and several others are whispering together. I hope that none of them gets sent out of class because today I really want everyone to stay where they are.

Miss Peabody pulls down the blinds and puts on the DVD of the documentary on India's sweatshops.

'Time for a nap!' says Lee, sinking down in his chair.

Evie and I exchange glances. 'Do you think anyone will notice the jumper from Amelia's dad's collection?' I whisper.

'I really hope so,' Evie whispers back. 'It's about time that people realised where Plunkett gets his clothes from.' Evie and I have so far resisted the urge to tell people about the jumper as we don't want it to sound as though we are spreading malicious rumours.

'Stop whispering, girls!' says Miss Peabody. Amelia titters. But the superior smile is soon wiped off her face when a few minutes later Ellen suddenly calls out, 'Amelia, you've got that jumper! Rewind the tape, Miss! Look—that white jumper on the programme—it's the same as yours, isn't it, Amelia? The one in the sweatshop is the same as the jumper in your dad's collection, isn't it?'

Everyone stares hard at the screen, focusing on the boy with sores on his legs sewing buttons on to the white jumper.

There is some murmuring, and a lot of people twist round in their seats and stare at Amelia, who glares back at them defensively.

'There's nothing bad about my dad's clothes—Jadene wears them! It's not the same jumper!' she squeals.

'Yes it is!' Ellen insists. It seems that other people have also seen Amelia wearing the white jumper and they nod in agreement.

'You'd better admit it, Amelia,' says

Salma. 'It is the same.'

Amelia opens her mouth, and closes it again. Then she gets up and rushes out of the room. Miss Peabody tells Jemima to go after her and make sure she is all right.

*　　*　　*

On our way to the drama studio for the lunchtime rehearsal and after thoroughly checking that Liam is nowhere in sight, I give the school tree a hug and reassure it that Evie and I are going to raise loads of money for Tree-aid to help its relations in the rainforest and help save the planet.

'Stop it, Lola,' laughs Evie, half embarrassed. 'Leave that poor tree alone. Come on! I want to see if any more people are going to turn up for the rehearsal.'

'I hope Amelia's OK,' I say. 'Did you see the expression on her face when she ran out of the room. She looked really upset. Jemima said she went home.'

Evie looks at me. 'The strange thing

183

is that I didn't actually want Amelia to be upset—I really don't want to be mean. I was more concerned about exposing the fact that her dad's clothes come from a sweatshop. If people like her dad go on importing clothes which are made in sweatshops like we saw on that programme, the sweatshops will continue to exist. It has to be stopped.'

'So it's nothing personal against Amelia.'

'No—I feel sorry for her, in a way. She's obviously loyal to her dad and loves him—but she shouldn't tell lies, or ignore the truth.'

*　　　*　　　*

The drama studio is packed with people. It seems that everyone has been talking about the sweatshop programme and the white jumper. With the exception of the So Cool Girls and one or two others, no one wants to model Amelia's dad's clothes any longer. Amelia has lost credibility—people are also disgusted that she lied to them about Jadene.

Evie is craning her neck and searching the room. 'I can't see Jack,' she says. 'I wonder where he is.'

'Hiding, I expect,' I comment. 'He let Amelia boss him around just so that he could get to see Jadene—or that's what he thought. It wasn't exactly cool behaviour, was it?'

'Oh, look!' I say, nudging Evie. 'There he is, in the doorway.'

A number of other people have noticed Jack, and they turn to look at him. Jack seizes his chance to make an entrance, wearing his dark glasses.

'The Jack
Is back!'

If he is expecting a round of applause, he doesn't get one.

'Oh—hello, Jack,' says Evie, coolly. 'What do you want?'

Jack looks at her uncertainly. He takes off his dark glasses. 'Er, I was wondering if you still need me in the show?'

'Yes we do. But why were you hanging around with Amelia?' says Evie, fixing her green eyes on him and putting him on the spot.

Jack hesitates, looking less cool than usual. 'She was a bit . . . er . . . bossy,' he falters. 'She kept following me—wouldn't leave me alone! It's a lot more fun being here with everyone.'

Suddenly Evie's face breaks into a smile. 'Jack—you're hired!' she says.

Jack grins, and does a few street dance moves.

'I'm Jack
And I'm back
You're talking to the man
With the plan
For saving the trees
And the birds and the bees!'

'And the frogs and the parrots!' adds Eddie.

Everyone laughs. Miss Peabody applauds. Then she calls for quiet and, for once, everyone stops talking and listens.

'It's wonderful to have so many of you here today!' she trills. 'But we've got a lot of work to do—the dress rehearsal will take place the day after tomorrow, and the following day it will be the show itself! I'm sure it's going to be a great show which will raise lots of money for Tree-aid!'

Everyone cheers.

'So let's get this show on the road!' Miss Peabody shouts in her squeaky voice. 'Jack! Will you run through your lovely introductory rap, please?'

*　　　*　　　*

As we are walking home later, arm in arm, I say to Evie, 'Today was so cool—apart from Amelia getting so upset. I don't feel good about that.'

'Oh, she'll bounce back!' says Evie. 'She's like a human rubber ball!'

'But everything else is great,' I continue. 'The rehearsal went really well. In fact, I don't see how it can get any better.'

Evie gives me a sideways look, her lips twitching in a slight smile. 'We'll see,' she says.

Eco-info

About half of the world's species of plants, animals and micro-organisms will be destroyed or severely threatened over the next 25 years due to the destruction of the rainforests.

CHAPTER SEVENTEEN

It's the dress rehearsal.

Jack, wearing a white shirt, black suit and his dark glasses, is standing on the stage with his back to the audience, ready to rehearse his introduction to the show for the last time before the actual event. Suddenly he swivels round dramatically, points to the audience and announces:

'Ladies and gentlemen
Welcome to this celebration
Please give us your consideration—and your cash!
Because if all the trees are gone
We'll have no planet left to live on!
Don't let global warming win
So let our show begin!'

There is a burst of clapping from the other acts who are sitting where the audience will be sitting tomorrow evening, and Megan and Tegan call out, 'Go, Jack!' Someone at the back of the hall carries on clapping when everyone else has stopped. We turn to see who it is, and Miss Peabody raises her finger to her lips to say 'ssh!'. But then we see who it is . . .

'MR WOODSAGE!'

He is still on crutches and wearing a neck brace, but he has a huge smile on his face.

'Mr Woodsage!' Evie and I run to greet him, followed by Miss Peabody, fluttering her hands like little pink fans.

'Mr Woodsage! How lovely to see you—what a lovely surprise!' Miss Peabody squeals. 'I wasn't expecting you. Did you get the invitation to come to the school tomorrow evening?'

'Yes, I did. It sounded very mysterious! Oh dear—have I spoilt the surprise?'

'It doesn't matter! We're just happy to see you. Welcome to our dress rehearsal for "Let Me Green-tertain You"! It's a show to raise money for Tree-aid—it was Lola and Evie's idea—and these are the Green-tertainers . . .' Miss Peabody indicates the other acts, who are all smiling broadly and crowding around to greet

190

Mr Woodsage.

Mr Woodsage is visibly moved. He sits down with Miss Peabody to watch the rehearsal while Evie and I introduce the acts.

When it is time for Evie to play 'Greensleeves' she has a sudden attack of nerves. 'My hands are shaking!' she hisses at me. 'How can I play the guitar?'

'You'll be fine!' I say reassuringly, giving her a hug. 'Go on!'

I introduce Evie, and she manages to play 'Greensleeves' all the way through very quickly.

'I always do things quickly when I'm nervous,' she says, talking fast and grinning as she comes off stage to a round of applause, and a cheer from Mr Woodsage.

The rest of the rehearsal runs smoothly, apart from a slight upset when Salma nearly falls off the stage— she teeters on the edge looking alarmed. Everyone gasps, and someone shouts 'No!' But fortunately she recovers her balance just in time.

'Phew!' Evie exclaims. 'That was

close! I'm nervous enough already!'

I look at her, puzzled. 'But you've played "Greensleeves", I say. 'You can stop feeling nervous now. Or are you already nervous about tomorrow?'

Evie doesn't reply. But she keeps looking round towards the main hall doors.

Lee makes everyone laugh when he appears dressed as a tree—he has found a proper tree costume complete with foliage—and grabs a microphone. 'Hello to all my adoring fans!' he shouts. 'I'm a celebri-TREE!'

Everyone groans.

Mr Woodsage loves Rico the parrot and Norman the tree frog. Eddie is careful not to push Norman on his skateboard anywhere near the edge of the stage.

Girls United sing in tune, and Firedance have perfected their routine so that they spell out *TREE AID* correctly first time. Mr Woodsage cheers.

Evie seems increasingly agitated.

'What is it?' I ask, impatiently. She is beginning to make me nervous!

Suddenly Evie leaps to her feet, and seconds later so does everyone else. Liam has just come into the hall with his band, and they are all carrying their instruments—apart from the drummer, obviously. The drums are already on stage, as they were used by another boy who played with the guitarist.

The Rock Hyraxes are going to play at the talent show!

'You knew about this, didn't you?' I exclaim, giving Evie a friendly push. 'It was your idea!'

Evie's eyes are shining. 'He took a lot of persuading,' she says. 'Liam isn't really into trees—and he was worried about being in a show with a load of Year Eights—but I wore him down!'

The Rock Hyraxes get on stage and play and everyone is cheering. They play an encore. When they have finished, Mr Woodsage says, 'What an amazing band! And what a wonderful show—so many talented people!'

He is right. We have come a long way since Jamie and Oliver did their impression of a balloon bursting. They have not been back since the chocolate ran out!

Mr Woodsage says that he hopes that it isn't necessary to choose a winning act, as he couldn't possibly choose—everyone is so good. Miss Peabody assures him that it isn't a competition, just an opportunity for everyone to show off their various talents.

Most of the rest of the school are crowding around the doorway in the main hall, attracted by hearing The Rock Hyraxes play, and there is a buzz of excitement.

'I bet we get a big audience tomorrow night!' Evie says to me excitedly.

I have spotted Amelia standing sulkily nearby, arms folded, glaring at us.

'I hope you're pleased with what's happened,' she snaps. 'My dad's show is wrecked—he's had to cancel the whole thing because that awful Wanda woman from the *Shrubberylands Sentinel* turned up at our house asking awkward questions and threatening to write a stupid article about my dad's clothes coming from sweatshops—and we know she's a friend of yours!'

'Wanda isn't awful,' says Evie. 'It's the sweatshops that are awful. Wanda just wants people to know the truth, like we do.'

Amelia glowers at us. 'It wasn't even my dad's fault—he gets the clothes through a middleman. So he didn't know they came from a sweatshop. But you've just gone and ruined everything!'

Slinging her schoolbag over her shoulder and giving us one last I-hate-you look, she marches away, followed by Jemima and one or two of the Not Quite So Cool As They Were Girls, who also give us Amelia-style nasty looks.

As we walk to the first of our afternoon lessons we see people using the school's new recycling bins—they are positioned in a corner of the main courtyard.

'That's good,' says Evie. 'But there's still work to be done turning the school green. I definitely think we should have a school vegetable plot, and some more

195

trees.'

Evie looks thoughtful. 'Do you believe Amelia?' she asks. 'Do you believe that her dad didn't know that the clothes came from sweatshops?'

'No,' I reply, with a sigh. 'I think that's what Amelia wants to believe.'

Eco-info

As their homeland is destroyed, the native peoples of the rainforests are also disappearing. It is estimated that there were 10 million people living in the Amazonian rainforest 500 years ago. Now there are fewer than 200,000. Their knowledge of the medicinal uses of rainforest plants and creatures is also being lost.

CHAPTER EIGHTEEN

The main hall is packed. In the doorway a few of the Green-tertainers are shaking and rattling Tree-aid collecting tins and buckets, which are already filling up with coins. They are also selling plenty of *Make Deforestation History* wristbands.

Standing just inside the entrance is Kate Meadowsweet from the Eco Gardens, holding Mr Macawber, the splendid parrot, who attracts a lot of attention. He and Rico, the African Grey parrot, start calling to each other. Other keepers have brought in Monty the royal python and Dave the chameleon, and Kate is explaining to people how these beautiful creatures will become extinct in the wild if they lose their rainforest habitat. People crowd around exclaiming, 'Oh! Cute!' although a few people edge away from the snakes, and Evie's mum, who has a bird phobia, keeps her distance from Mr Macawber. Then Kate and the keepers take the animals out after we have thanked her very much for bringing them in.

The show begins. MC Jack's rap makes everyone clap. Lee gets plenty of laughs. Shaheen dances beautifully, like an exotic butterfly. The singers are in tune, the dancers are in step and Miss Peabody is in raptures. Everyone roars with laughter when Rico the parrot flies out from the stage over the heads of the audience and lands on Mrs Balderdash's head. Norman the skateboarding tree frog is a star— everyone holds their breath as he trundles slowly across the stage, bathed in a single spotlight.

I notice that many people in the audience approach Evie's mum in the interval—so I think that we have helped drum up some business for her by wearing our Fashion Passion clothes! We have also stirred up business for Meltonio, who is selling his ice-creams during the interval at a table at the back of the hall. Beaming from ear to ear, he tells us that, thanks to us, his ice-cream will be available in the school canteen from next week in three flavours: Vitamin-enriched Vanilla, Sugar-free Strawberry and Healthy-choice Chocolate.

Also for sale during the interval are compostable water bottles, manufactured from corn, although they look like ordinary plastic. These are wasted on most of the parents who prefer the glasses of wine which are also on offer.

The second half of the show soars to a dizzy height when, towards the end, The Rock Hyraxes take to the stage and raise the school roof—people start dancing on their chairs. I am relieved that Mum and Dad, Evie's mum and dad and Wanda remain seated—although Evie's parents cheer louder than anyone! Evie and I hug each other in excitement.

When everyone has calmed down, Mr Woodsage gives a speech of thanks, with particular thanks to Evie and me for having the idea to put on a show for Tree-aid, and he gives a short talk about Tree-aid and how it is helping to stop deforestation.

Mrs Balderdash thanks the Green-tertainers for a wonderful show, and announces proudly that the school has decided to plant some more trees in the grounds.

'That's so cool!' Evie exclaims, her eyes shining.

'Yes,' I agree. 'The trees will encourage more birds into the school, too.'

Miss Peabody then makes a short speech, in which she thanks Evie and me personally for coming up with the idea for the talent show, putting it together and having the courage and determination to go ahead with it despite problems and setbacks along the way. Everyone claps and cheers and Evie and I glow with a mixture of pride and embarrassment, as everyone is looking at us on the stage taking a bow. Miss Peabody adds that she hopes that the Green-tertainers will put on more shows in the future, in aid of other charities. There is a fresh burst of clapping and cheering.

'That was amazing!' I exclaim, as we leave the hall, passing the rattling

Tree-aid collecting tins and buckets which are filling up fast. 'I'm glad Mrs Balderdash is having more trees planted. Now the school tree won't be lonely any more! It's going to have some friends.'

'Yes, Lola!' says Evie, patting my head teasingly. 'Are you going to give your tree friend a hug?'

'No!' I retort, feeling embarrassed in case people overhear and think I am weird.

'Well, I am!' says a voice just behind me. It is Liam! I notice that he is wearing a *Make Deforestation History* wristband.

In front of everyone he runs across the main courtyard and throws his arms around the school tree! The other members of The Rock Hyraxes laugh and call out 'Tree-hugger!' But Liam doesn't seem to mind any longer. 'I've realised how important trees are!' he says, coming over and putting his arms round Evie and me. 'Thanks for getting me and the band involved,' he says. 'It was a cool show!' Then he goes off with his friends.

I float home in a dream. Liam hugged me! He hugged a tree—and then he hugged Evie and me! I have been hugged before by Liam—once—when he played with his band at the Eco Gardens. So maybe it doesn't matter—maybe he wouldn't mind if I hugged him occasionally! Maybe I don't need to worry . . . although I am an eco-worrier.

We are walking home with a crowd of other people who are heading in the same direction. Mum and Dad and Evie's parents are being non-eco-friendly and driving home. Someone walks past Evie and gives her a pat on the shoulder.

'You were great!' he says.

It is Ben from Year Ten . . .

*   *   *

'He noticed I exist!' sighs Evie, who is lying on my bed, smiling an 'in love' smile and not really concentrating on anything I say. I am beginning to regret inviting her for a sleepover.

'Yes—he noticed you exist,' I say,

202

taking a sip of my organic raspberry smoothie—I persuaded Mum to get organic smoothies for Evie and me. 'It doesn't mean you're going to get married and live happily ever after.' I attempt to change the subject. 'The show was so cool—everyone loved Norman, and it was so funny when Rico landed on Mrs Balderdash's head—did you see the expression on her face? She looked so startled! I think we raised loads of money for Tree-aid, and we certainly raised awareness. I'm sure a lot of people will go away and plant trees and really think about how important trees are to the whole planet, and how deforestation must be stopped. I couldn't believe it when Liam hugged the school tree! Isn't it great that the school is going to plant more trees? Evie? Evie—are you listening?'

'He noticed I exist!'

THWUMMPP! I hit her with a pillow . . .